Convoluted Tales

J.P. Johnson

Lost Lake Folk Art

SHIPWRECKT BOOKS PUBLISHING COMPANY

IN®
DIE

Minnesota

Cover art and interior design by Shipwreckt Books
Original photo used on the cover from NOAA
Photo Library, NOAA Central Library;
OAR/ERL/National Severe Storms Laboratory
(NSSL), taken near Cordell, Oklahoma, May 22,
1981.

Forty-seven years cold first appeared in the May 2014
issue of *Lost Lake Folk Opera* magazine.

For my second-grade teacher, Rose Blumenson, who taught me how to read and write, and to my wife, Marylee, for giving me a couple of good story lines.

Thank you to the members of the Minneapolis Writers' Workshop who keep me writing, and thank you to publisher and editor, Tom Driscoll, for your editing skills and introducing me to the world of publishing.

Table of Contents

I f you looked at a map of Minnesota, you wouldn't find the town of Center City because it doesn't exist … not anymore.

As a kid, I had heard stories of the town up north that had disappeared before the start of the Civil War. I had some business dealings in that area in the afternoon and since I'd be taking State Highway 371, it wouldn't hurt to check it out. History had always interested me.

I heard there was a highway rest stop halfway between Fort Ripley and Brainerd, the exact location where Center City once stood. Curious to see if some of the stories were true, I planned to stop there to see if there was any official documentation.

In 1858, when statehood for Minnesota was ratified, a group of citizens from Center City petitioned the government to move its capital to the geographic center of the state: Center City, Crow Wing County. They reasoned that being in the center of the state; it would be easier for legislators to travel from all over the state, whether by horse and buggy, stagecoach or rail, since they had a spacious, newly-constructed depot.

A couple of months later, the state got around to sending them a telegraphed, terse reply: "No, too small." The capital would remain in Saint Paul, formerly known as Pig's Eye. Legislators could have their choice of several fine hotels within the city limits of Saint Paul. They could also travel by horse and buggy, stagecoach or rail.

O n May seventeenth, 1859, the Norwegian population of Center City began a three-day festival to celebrate *Syttende Mai*. For no apparent reason, a few Germans joined in the celebration. Beer, whiskey, wine and akevitt were enthusiastically chugged in all five of the city's saloons.

Suddenly, the wind died, the birds stopped chirping and the sky turned a yellowish green. Following the Mississippi River, a monstrous tornado climbed from the river bank to the southwest of Center City. People in the saloons heard the noise and gathered by the doors and windows to gaze as if hypnotized by its undulating dance.

"Py yimminy, lookit dat ting!" the mayor exclaimed before he and five others were sucked up into its maw. The tornado then split into three and savaged the rest of the town, its citizens and livestock including old man Swenson's cow while Mrs. Swenson was milking it. The school bell rang fitfully before it was torn from its foundation. Fortunately, there were no children inside because it was closed for the holiday. Debris from the hotel, which was built in anticipation for housing state legislators, was found east of town. And the handsome, new railroad depot, which would've brought lawmakers from every part of the state to Center City, lay in ruins.

Before the end of that fateful day, the few hundred survivors from a population of 1,200, were tallying their dead.

The town of Brainerd sent an emissary to the former Center City for the purpose of inviting the survivors to become members of its community. He promised a train would pick them up and whatever remained of their belongings.

Time and the elements had now taken everything and didn't leave a trace. Nature had reclaimed the land and Center City had disappeared.

When I arrive at the rest stop, I see a bronze plaque on the wall commemorating the seven-hundred fifty people who perished at that exact location of *Syttende Mai* in 1859.

A large, red-faced, civil service attendant watches people as they mill around waiting to use the restrooms or push coins into vending machines. Then, he invites the group of about ten adults and children to look out the back window. There's a clearing in the woods: a square cemetery with flat, granite markers. They're not the original headstones but, the attendant tells the group, it is in fact, the original cemetery.

"You folks can at least go out there and look at the markers," the attendant bellows and sarcastically adds, "you don't have to be in such a hurry all the time, you're not that important!"

Most of the group take offense and head for their cars. The few remaining eventually leave too. I go outside simply to placate the mounting fury of the attendant.

Outside, standing by one of the markers is a short, gaunt man. His dirty, gray clothes drape from his shoulders as if hanging on a wire coat hanger. A large, black fedora is pulled down to his eyebrows so that he tilts his head back in order to look at me. The skin on his face is stretched tight making him look more skeletal than humanly possible.

He cocks his head toward a marker. "Look at this headstone," he says. I read the name: *Anders Pederson, Born June 2, 1851, Died May 17, 1859.* "His body was found in the school basement after the tornado hit," the man continues.

"I thought the school had closed that day," I tell the man who looks more like a spectral being.

"It *was* closed that day, but me and the boy were in the basement. I killed him. Choked him with these hands." He holds out his long, boney fingers and wrings an imaginary neck.

"Why? Why would you do that?"

"I was the school's janitor, so I seen him almost every day. He was a good-looking boy, that Anders. Anyway, I was doing some work in the school, seen him walking by and told him to come inside. Told him I wanted to show him something. We went in the basement and told him that I wanted to have sex with him and he started screaming real loud. I got scared and choked him to death. Then, the tornado hit."

"Why are you telling me this?"

"'Cause nobody knows I killed the boy and I want you to tell somebody."

"That's a pretty good story," pretending that I believe him. Of course, I laugh, shattering the illusion. "If you're acting like a ghost, in which I don't believe, you still deserve an Oscar, but I don't have one, so I'll give you ten dollars instead."

"Thanks mister. Make sure you tell the guy in that building about my killing that boy 'cause nobody knows, okay?"

"Oh, I will. Don't worry."

3

I walk back to the building as the attendant comes out of his office. "I have to tell you about the guy out there who says that he killed a kid before the tornado struck. I felt sorry for him and gave him some money."

"What guy?" he looks out the window, "there's no guy out there. Listen, you must've hit your head on the urinal while you were lookin' down at your pecker. I saw you standin' out there by yourself. Now, get outta here before I throw you out!"

oldier

he night sky is beginning to clear, exposing near and distant stars. You're hopeful that maybe tomorrow, if it doesn't start raining again, your outfit can move forward. Until then, you're stuck for the third consecutive night, in the same foxhole, which you'd dug in the mud three days ago. Although it's not raining anymore, the inside of your hiding place, your foxhole, is still wet. You spread your rain poncho out, partly on the ground and partly on the wall. You place the heels of your boots in the same, small gouges in the dirt, lean back and brace yourself against the wall. You think it's rather amusing that you alternately have trouble sleeping, as well as staying awake. But, you *have* to stay awake to survive.

You position yourself so that the rim of your foxhole is at eye level. You pull the bolt back on your M1 and expertly slam a round into the chamber. As you light a cigarette, carefully cupping the flame of your lighter, you know that you have all night to look at the stars and dream of home.

You wonder what your family's doing right now, so you take out a slightly creased photo of your wife and son. You know that he's older now. He was two when the picture was taken and since you've been gone for two years ... your thoughts trail off to the time you last saw them, seeing you off at the train depot. Your mom and dad were there, too. Your mom was crying her eyes out, as usual, when she gave you one of her soft, warm hugs and a gentle kiss on your cheek. Your dad was more formal; a firm handshake, a pat on the back and the parting words, "Give 'em hell, soldier!" Then, you turned to your wife, Doris. You both had tears in your eyes and you both wished that you didn't have to go and you both wished that your embrace would last forever.

At least, you got to bring the scent of her perfume with you, if only briefly. Your little boy, imitating your dad, solemnly shook your hand. You bent down and he kissed you on the cheek.

You glanced over at the conductor. He scowled at you, looked at his pocket watch and growled, "Board!"

5

One last kiss from Doris before you hoisted your duffel bag to your shoulder and climbed onto the train. You saw that your dad had lifted your son, Chris, and held him in his arms.

They were all smiling and waving, except that your dad's smile looked strained, more like a grimace.

You think of the photograph of your dad, framed, hand-tinted in pastels, on the end table in your parents' living room. He's a smiling doughboy with his campaign hat cocked on the side of his head. That was a war which took place a generation before.

In the picture, your dad was younger than you are now. It was taken before he married your mom and before he shipped off to France. He said his goodbyes at the same train station and promised to write soon, just as you have said. You figured that you had some time to write letters while on the train and after you got to Fort Dix. *Write to your in-laws first. Get it over with*.

You didn't know it at the time, that you'd be sent to Europe to fight the Germans in another war they were calling, World War II. Your dad called it, round two; same enemy, same reasons.

He didn't talk about it much, but he was in the Marine 2nd Division at the bloodbath they called, The Battle of Belleau Wood. You found some selfish solace in the fact that you didn't have to balance on the same narrow line between life and death as did your dad.

You're not involved in a fierce battle with a strong, heavily-armed enemy. Presently, they're calling it a mop-up operation. They tell you that the Krauts are, "weakened and on the run."

It's only taken two months for the Fifth Army to secure a foothold in Southern Italy and send the enemy running north. The Germans were chased out of Salerno and that's where you are, in your foxhole, in the Spring of 1944.

You're attached to the Fifth Army, under the command of Lieutenant General Mark Clark, but you never actually saw him.

You take a swig of water from your canteen, light another cigarette and wait patiently for the pinkish glow of pre-dawn. You hear, in the far distance, muffled cannon fire, but not the closer rifle fire that you heard on the first two nights. This makes you uncomfortable and a wave of apprehension sweeps over you because you know that there are German snipers still nearby.

They've fallen behind for a purpose and the lack of rifle fire, means that they could only be waiting and planning … thinking of doing something. So, you find yourself becoming fearful of what you don't hear.

You look up and see wispy clouds crossing over a quarter-moon.

You were told that some German soldiers, especially snipers, who infiltrated behind enemy lines, were taught American idiom, without a trace of a German accent. Sometimes at night, you could hear them. They'd cry out, painfully, "Medic, over here, hurry!" Or, "Hey, G.I., got a cigarette?" They'd also yell, "Joe, c'mere!" Apparently, Joe is their default name for an American soldier. Of course, you knew better than to respond. Those who did, usually got picked-off with a single shot. That thought makes you grip your carbine tightly.

Every few minutes, you scan the surrounding area. No sounds. It's a still night, with no wind to stir the leaves on the trees. When you think that in every war, the War Department tells the troops and tells them every year, that they'll be home by Christmas, it makes you sigh.

Someone close breaks your reverie and whispers, "Hello, Joe." It comes from behind you. You spin around, but you're too slow. A Kraut sniper is crouched on one knee, just a few feet away, his eyes wild with excitement, shouldering his Mauser and taking aim.

You hear the acute crack of a rifle shot. You dive to the bottom of your foxhole.

You're amazed that you're not hit. But, you stay there, not daring to move.

Suddenly, you hear someone laugh and shout, "I got him, I got him!" You lie still. You don't know who's yelling. You hear footsteps of a couple of guys and some incoherent mumbling. Then, one of them says, "We got him, come out and see." You rise slowly, with your M1 ready.

"Take it easy," they laugh because they can see that your hands are shaking. They explain that they were watching him for a while and as he crept closer, they decided that the optimum time had come to bring the sniper's career to an end. The three of you laugh as you look down at the German. You slap the back of the comrade who fired the shot and say, "Thanks, buddy!" A single bullet hole had pierced the left side of his helmet. It looks as though the sniper had only fallen over on his side. His eyes are still wide-open. You can't see any blood, but you know that he's dead.

"Better him than you," one of them remarks. You laugh nervously in response and say, "Yeah, it's much better this way." Laughter turns to silence. "Lucky bastard," you mutter, "at least this goddam war's over for him."

lmost forgotten

fter a week of steady, cold rain, that September afternoon turned out to be gorgeous, upper 70s, the sky, a canopy of luminous turquoise with a few high, wispy clouds. Perfect for any kind of an outdoor game.

I was on my way to work. I laughed when I thought about the word, "work". All I was going to do, was get dressed up and walk around the sports bar, patting the backs of good old boys, who sat at the bar, shaking hands with others and wandering from table to table, like a troubadour, asking patrons if they were "enjoying their dinners?" and "is everything to your satisfaction?"

People thought that I owned the bar when it was actually owned by a consortium of men who used professional athletes to front their enterprises. They owned a string of places like this, all across the country; all named after some has-been ballplayer, or broken-down boxer. We were all paid pretty well for the use of our names. In my case, they handed me $50,000, put my name on a sign, along with a cartoon caricature of myself. In return, I was asked to spend a couple of nights a week playing the part of a genial host. I was glad to oblige because, if I had any doubt that fans had forgotten about me, I was reassured that they hadn't. I know that it was just a feeble sense of insecurity. Unlike performers, such as movie actors, whose careers can span a lifetime and preserved on film for decades after they're dead, an athlete can sometimes have only a finite existence.

It had been nearly twenty years since I retired from the NFL. I considered it an unremarkable, twelve-season career. Ten years with the Rams and two with the Vikings. I was lucky not to have suffered any serious injuries which, of course, abruptly ended the careers of some running backs. I had minor injuries; ankle sprains, a hyper-extended elbow, hamstring pulls, broken fingers and a broken nose.

Ray Norman broke my nose. It was an away game at Lambeau Field: Packers versus Rams; a cold dreary November day with low-

9

hanging, threatening clouds. I played fullback and on that particular play, I'd lead-block for a hotshot, rookie tailback, swinging around right end. Before we lined up, I advised him to slow down, wait for my block and try not to run up my back. We were both running along the sideline. I was only two steps ahead, when out of the corner of my eye, I saw Norman come lumbering toward us, focused on destroying the guy I was supposed to protect. He didn't even seem to notice me. As he was about to move past, I blind-sided him with my shoulder and forearms. It only made him teeter off balance, but it did make him miss the tackle and my rookie gained eight yards before he was shoved out-of-bounds. Then, I saw Norman jumping around, waving his arms, growling at the ref for not calling a clip.

"He clipped me and you know it!" His fists were doubled up, his face crimson with rage and as he turned toward me, shouting, "Next time, thirty-three!"

"Yeah, next time, sixty-six!"

I didn't really clip him. What he probably felt was my shoulder and elbow glancing off his back.

At six-four, two hundred thirty-seven pounds, I was about Norman's size, but was much faster. I guess it was my speed which kept me from being chosen as one of those marshmallow linemen in high school and college. On the other hand, Ray Norman was chosen to be a linebacker, mostly because he was smaller than a lineman, but mostly because he was a goddam animal!

I hated to lead-block, even though I enjoyed knocking tough looking, little cornerbacks out of their shoes. I preferred to take a screen pass and run up the sideline or, putting my head down and plowing through the line.

My number was called in the huddle. Take the handoff and plow off left tackle. Norman met me at the line, like he was psychic and it was his turn to plow. He was never content with crashing into ball carriers, he'd keep driving them into the ground until the whistle blew. He had knocked me on my ass and was lying on top of me, when he grabbed a bar on my facemask and slid his first through, smashing my nose flat. He smiled and stated, matter-of-factly, "The ref didn't see that one either."

After that game and the following seasons, I had a vertical bar added to my facemask. They call it a half-cage, designed to keep animals out.

The numbers and names of the Packers blur in my memory, except for Ray Norman.

I could've retired in California or Nevada, where I grew up, but I still seemed to be a popular figure among Minnesota sports fans. They put a sincere effort into being appreciative during my playing days and even now, I continue to feel it. It's not adoration, it's appreciation. And they don't even notice that I put on a little weight. A little weight? I'm close to three hundred pounds and probably shrunk a couple of inches!

I, the formerly great, Brad Vanderhaven, drove through town toward the sport bar which bore my name. Next to the front door, was a parking spot with my name on it, of course.

The day manager greeted me, all smiles, with an announcement of great import, "Boss, look what came in the mail! Hope you don't mind, but I opened it."

Astonished at who'd sent it, I stared at it for a few seconds. It was a framed black and white glossy photo, 14½ by 18½, under plexiglass, of a vicious-looking Ray Norman in a Packers uniform. At the bottom, written in his own beefy hand, "Best Wishes, Your Friend, Ray Norman."

I said, "Hang it by the bar. We open in a half-hour and I want the customers to see it."

"Something else came with it; an envelope, Boss."

It was a sealed envelope which I hastily ripped open and read just five words, "Sorry, I broke your nose."

hat late morning was unseasonably pleasant for the third of August in Minnesota. The sun arced toward its apex on that cloudless day. From her home on Chalmers Road and Oak Place, seventeen-year-old Barbara Lynn Baker walked three blocks north on Chalmers to Eighth Avenue. A neighbor waved and shouted, "Hi."

Barbara returned the wave and continued walking west on Eighth. She passed her high school, Columbia Hills Senior High, on her way to visit a friend, Kathy Thompson, who lived on Fillmore Street. It was exactly one mile from her house to her friend's. She and her parents were planning to go on vacation later that afternoon. She assured them that she would be home in time and that it was a nice enough day to walk back home. Her parents began to worry when late morning turned to afternoon and afternoon turned to early evening, Barbara failed to return home. They called the Thompson house and Kathy told them she had left a long time ago; about one o'clock.

On that Thursday evening at 6:00 p.m., her parents phoned the Columbia Hills police to report their daughter missing and left a description. Their worry increased to near panic.

A barely traceable rain fell during the night.

Friday, August fourth at 10:40 a.m., the police department in the neighboring city of Freemont, received a phone call, an anonymous tip from a man between eighteen and thirty-five who evidently was trying to disguise his voice. "You have a body in Freemont." The caller gave detailed instructions as to its exact location.

Chief Ed McCullum, Inspector Don Willard and Sergeant Herb Vollner, began a short search along a winding road in a wooded area, commonly referred to as a "lovers lane". There, they found a girl's body, nude from the waist down, wearing only a white t-shirt, throat cut and stabbed four times in the abdomen. There were no bruises on the victim, but there were slash wounds on her back and arms. She lay, in full rigor, on her right side, with her left leg bent at a forty-five-degree angle. Her head rested in a dark pool of thickened blood.

On August ninth, the *Columbia Hills Observer*, a local weekly newspaper, ran a 48-point headline on the front page: BRUTAL MURDER OF LOCAL GIRL DISCOVERED IN LOVERS LANE

Her shorts and underwear had been removed, leading investigators to speculate whether or not she'd been sexually assaulted. The Andrews County crime lab would make that determination. Also found at the scene was a kitchen butcher knife with an eight-inch blade. Both her shorts and the knife were found near her body.

Now a heavily industrialized area, in 1967, Lovers lane was a wooded area north of 19th Avenue east of River Road.

Subsequent small newspaper articles that August reported the partial crime lab results: there was no presence of drugs or alcohol in her body, and the blood on the knife was Barbara's. The *Observer*'s last issue in August, featured an interview with a forensic psychiatrist, a "profiler" who suggested that the killer may not have been a sexual psychopath.

Investigators from the Andrews County Sheriff's Office, Freemont P.D. and Columbia Hills P.D. began questioning her friends, her classmates, her teachers and area residents. They stated that she was a good girl who didn't seem to have any enemies. Her classmates, from her junior year, said that although she was popular, she wasn't going steady with any boys. In fact, they said, she wasn't dating anyone. Freemont Police Chief McCullum stated that they had several leads, but had no one in custody.

Neighbors living near the crime scene didn't hear any screams or, saw the girl enter the woods.

Because there were no scuff marks on the ground and that she had completely bled out where she lay, it was apparent that she had been murdered where she was found.

Freemont police identified the body by her Columbia Hills class ring with the initials B. B. on it. They notified the Columbia Hills P.D. who in turn, gave a matching description of the girl who'd been reported missing the day before.

The victim of this heinous crime was not only Barbara, but her parents and her three younger brothers.

She was a very attractive brunette, popular at school, a good student and at seventeen, had already exhibited the self-assuredness of an adult. She had just had her birthday the month before and was looking forward to the 1967- 68 school year ... her senior year. Perhaps she planned to continue her involvement in extra-curricular activities; helping edit the school newspaper, being a member of the Girls' Athletic Association, The Political Forum Club and being a majorette with the marching band.

Monday, August seventh, Barbara's funeral and burial took place at the prestigious Elmwood Cemetery in South Minneapolis. Her funeral wasn't held at her church and there were two large cemeteries closer to the suburb of Columbia Hills. This struck many people as an odd choice.

The Freedom of Information Act was passed in 1998, leading to dozens of inquiries into the thirty-one-year-old cold case murder of Barbara Lynn Baker.

That same year, the cold case became active and was assigned to two investigators of the Andrews County Criminal Investigations Division. Twelve years later, they had retired.

CID Captain Frank Crowley left a message for Lieutenants Cheryl Atkinson and Byron Smith to see him in his office—first thing in the morning.

The door to Crowley's office was open and the two detectives stood nervously in the doorway. Smith's 6'5" frame dwarfed his diminutive partner. Without looking up, Crowley said, "Come in," and motioned for them to sit down at the two chairs in front of his metal desk. On the desk was a brown, bulging, accordion file. Crowley pushed it toward them and sat back, his eyes fixed on the file, then sitting forward, finally looked at them. "This, people, is the Barbara Lynn Baker murder file. Unsolved, but active. Congratulations, you've been selected to handle it, now." He smirked at their surprised expressions. "You folks are the new team."

Atkinson spoke, first. "We've both got big caseloads and now this?"

15

"Hey," Crowley said, "you can take care of those first. This case is not a priority, but the girl's mother and brothers are still alive and it's got to look like we're continuing to do everything possible to solve it."

"Nothing new since 1967?" Smith asked.

"That's right. One time we had three solid suspects. One died in Viet Nam, the other two in car accidents. Nothing there. They were in the wrong place at the wrong time. Two died before the murder and the other one was out of state at the time. We've also done a lot of DNA, but no matches from CODIS."

Crowley continued, "Then, this guy, Rod Hanson, wrote a novel, fictionalizing the case. It actually was pretty good. He used to be a crime reporter on TV and had interviewed one of the original investigators, Freemont Inspector Willard. Willard allowed Hanson to view the case file. You know, for background on police procedures. Now, listen to this. Before Willard died, he gave a copy of the file to Hanson. I got ahold of Hanson and told him, in no uncertain terms, to bring me his copy and that he's not allowed to have it because the case is active."

"Well, did he do that?" Atkinson asked, leaning forward in her chair, unconsciously causing Crowley to sit back.

"Yeah, but here's the thing. Because he was so smug and so cheerfully willing to hand it over, I thought that maybe he'd made another copy. Of course, he denied it. When we searched his house, we found it. It's all here; pictures and reports. Other stuff, gathered at the scene, is in the evidence room. Start on this when you have time." Crowley slapped his palms on the top of the desk, as if to rise, then sat back instead. "It's all yours, detectives. I want to be the first to know if you find anything."

Atkinson and Smith walked far enough down the hall to be out of Crowley's eavesdropping range. Smith leaned his shoulder against the wall and slid down to match Atkinson's eye level. He held the file in the crook of his other arm like a football. Atkinson faced him, arms akimbo.

"Do you want to get started on this now, Cheryl? Or, later."

"I'd rather get laid by my ex than work on this case."

Smith looked at her with a feigned expression of disdain. "I mean we've never worked together, so I don't know. Twice a week, maybe?"

"Too often, Byron. More like once a month. I propose the last Sunday of the month."

Byron laughed, turned his back to the wall and slid upward straightening his posture. "Well, Crowley said that it wasn't a priority and we both have other things to do."

"Tell me about it. When I first came to CID, the Barbara Baker case is all anybody talked about. That lasted for only a few months, now, it's suddenly important again. I have to admit that all the previous cases I've worked were easy. In comparison, this one looks impossible."

"I heard that the previous detectives were deluged with gangs of amateur sleuths as well as a few psychics. That's why the case was reactivated to stop that crap. Then, people started saying that it was a cover-up."

"Byron, forget that cover-up stuff. I don't care if our predecessors did absolutely nothing. We are going to work this until ... until there's nothing left we can do."

"You're the senior investigator, Cheryl. We'll do it your way, but I think that we should look for things everyone else overlooked ... even the most seemingly insignificant details."

"Okay, keep the file in your desk and I'll meet you on Sunday in two weeks."

Using the telephone code they devised, Barbara Baker called him, hanging up after one ring and calling back. "I've got to talk to you, right now. It's important!"

"Barb, what's the matter. What happened?"

"It's something I have to talk to you about ... in person."

"Okay, okay ..."

"Pick me up on the corner of Fourth and McKinley."

She waited only three minutes when the gray Chevy pulled up.

"Christ, Barb, are you sick? You don't look too good."

"Just drive away from here. Some place. Maybe over to the park."

"How about our usual place?"

"No, not there. What I have to say, will only take a few minutes."

"Okay, we'll park by the waterworks."

He looked at her quizzically. He'd never seen her this serious.

"I missed my period. I'm pretty sure I'm pregnant."

His faced turned ashen. "How do you know *I* did it? Besides, I always use condoms."

"It has to be you. I've never been with anybody else."

Anger mounting, "You'll have to get an abortion, that's all there is to it."

"I'm keeping it, even if I have to wait 'til next year to graduate. All I'm asking you to do is take responsibility and do the right thing."

"And the right thing, according to you, is to divorce my wife and leave her with two kids. Plus, they'll be warming up a cell for me at Stillwater. You're jailbait! All you're concerned about is sitting out another school year. I could lose everything...my job ... everything!"

"You should've thought about that before. I'll be eighteen next year and I'll graduate. You can marry me then. Will you do that for me?"

"That's a lot to think about, Barb. I just can't deal with it, now. I'm working second shift and have to go home and get ready for work. But, I promise I'll have answer for you as soon as I can."

It was late in December of 2010 when Atkinson and Smith spread the extensive case file and scarce pieces of evidence out on a conference table. They had agreed to meet the last Sunday of every month to go over the file. But, this was the third month. There was nothing new about what to discuss.

"Did we talk about that anonymous phone call?" Atkinson asked.

"Yeah, a couple of times. Why?"

"Well, there's one of two possible scenarios. One is, the killer taunting, 'catch me if you can' and the other is, a dumb, scared kid who found a dead body in the middle of the night."

"I could buy the second one. A boy drives in with a girl…"

"Or, boy," Atkinson adds.

"Never mind, Cheryl. He drives in with a girl. They're both underage, drinking, they freak-out and the boy waits 'til the next day to call. He didn't want to be suspected and probably was too scared, like you said."

"This was before 911," said Atkinson, "and emergency calls went directly to the station where they were automatically recorded. We still have the recording so, if it happens to be the first scenario and if we ever find the bastard, we can do a voice print, see if it matches and if there's any DNA, we can nail him."

"Sometimes I feel like we're just pissing in the wind, Cheryl."

"Think positive, will you?"

"Speaking of DNA traces, faint as they are, anything new?"

"Just partials, Byron. The wooden knife handle was so degraded, it had deep cracks in it. So, they thought they could extract DNA. The lab got some food bacteria and mold from the brass rivets, but no human DNA traces."

"With no DNA, Cheryl."

The detailed forensic pathology report indicated that she was 5'8", 113 pounds, good muscle tone associated with regular exercise. Lividity and body temperature revealed that the time of death was estimated at between 2 p.m. and 6 p.m. The knife slashes on her back and backs of her upper arms may mean that she was attacked from behind and that her throat was also cut from behind, carotid to carotid. There was also a deeper wound at the right carotid than at the left which may also indicate that the killer was left-handed and having the leverage of a taller person.

Since blood was found on her shorts, the shorts and underwear evidently were removed post-mortem. The four stab wounds to the abdomen were also committed post-mortem. She had not been sexually assaulted.

"Cheryl … everybody thinks that she was pregnant and that's why she was stabbed in the stomach."

"I thought so, too. But, it says that she wasn't. One thing that

I'm almost sure of, is that Miss Baker had a familiar relationship with her killer."

"Of course," Smith said, "she got into a car, willingly and knew exactly where she was going because she'd been there before. Probably many times. Cheryl, our non-dating girl was leading a double-life!"

"That does make sense, kid. I think after this case, I can happily retire."

The two detectives repeated the ritual of examining evidence once a month which usually ended in disappointing speculation. They mutually agreed, with the blessing of Capt. Crowley, that they would discuss the case only twice a year, thereafter.

Barbara Baker's phone rang once and stopped. She hurried to the phone and waited. Two seconds later, it rang again. It was him.

"Barb, I have to see you. I've reached a decision."

"Good. I'm going on vacation with my folks tomorrow, but I'll be going over to Kathy Thompson's first, around noon. You can call me there. Don't use the signal."

"What if Kathy answers?"

"So what? She doesn't know who you are."

"Okay. I'm working day shift. I'll have to think of something, in case I have to explain what I'm doing in Columbia Hills."

"Byron, do you realize it's been three years that we've been doing this? That makes this case unsolved for almost forty-seven years."

"Yeah, it'll probably stay unsolved for another forty-seven. I've about had it. We've gone over everything at least twenty times. The interviews with the classmates, teachers, neighbors, her parents … There wasn't much information coming from the second to the last one to see her alive. That Thompson girl."

"She was in shock, Byron. Somebody should've re-interviewed her later."

Smith picked up a clear, plastic bag with a large, pink comb in it and looked intensely at Cheryl. "Her parents identified it as

Barbara's by the two broken teeth. Her mother said that the teeth were broken because she always carried it in her back pocket. I know prints and DNA also confirm it was hers. But, I don't understand the significance of this piece of evidence and why we even have it."

"Because, Byron, my very good friend, it was discovered a week later and it was not found at the crime scene. That's why it's significant."

"Barb, it's for you. Some guy." Kathy smiled and winked. "How'd he know you were here?"

"Kathy, do you wanna back off a little? Give me some privacy? But, just stay where I can see you and don't go near the kitchen extension."

"Is there something going on with this guy, you're not telling me?" she smiles broadly and raises an eyebrow.

"Will you let me talk to him, Kathy, so I can find out?"

"Knock it off, Barb, and listen to me. I want you to leave in twenty minutes. There's a construction crew working at the high school and I don't think it's wise for anybody to see us together. Walk around the corner and come out on 8th and Tyler. That way, I'll see you from a block away and I'll pick you up."

She got into the car and he told her to keep her head down and strongly suggested that they drive to their usual place. No one else would be there on that weekday afternoon.

Barbara's soft, brown eyes met his as she asked the all-important question. "So, what're you gonna do? Leave your wife?"

"Why is it so goddam hot in this car?" he asked himself, "I gotta take this shirt off."

He removed his belt, placed it on the seat and lay his shirt on top of it. She got out to stretch in the sunshine.

"It's not hot," she said, without facing him, "it's gorgeous and so quiet out here."

"Hey, Barb! I got your answer!"

His face twisted and florid with rage, he began slashing at her back with a butcher knife.

"Oh, god! What're you doing?" She swung the back of her left hand, hitting him in the ribs and scratching the skin with her ring. She turned a little, but he was on her, grabbing the back of her hair, knife at her throat.

He cut swiftly and deeply. She gurgled a muffled scream that no one would hear, except the man killing her. She tried to stop the pulsing, gushing blood with her hands. He pushed her down and stood over her, panting and sweating. Only a few seconds later, it was over. Her lifeless body convulsed a couple of times.

Rolling her on her back, he pulled off her shorts, along with her underwear and cast them aside. *Gotta make it look like a different motive.*

There was blood, but he was surprised at how little blood had spattered on his bare chest and stomach. Admiring her nakedness only momentarily, he knew he had more work to do. Her unseeing eyes seemed to be watching him, as he knelt by her side.

"Pregnant, huh bitch?" he grunted.

With both hands on the knife handle, he raised it above his head and savagely plunged the blade down into her stomach. Repeating it three more times, for good measure, he whispered, "I guess you won't be wrecking my life, or anybody else's."

He turned her on her side and sank the knife blade into the ground. Then, reaching into his back pocket, he pulled out a handkerchief and wiped the handle and the splashes of blood from his chest. "What's that?" He straightened up, muscles tensed, hearing something rustling in the dry brush. "A squirrel, or rabbit, is all."

"Chief, come here!" the dispatcher called, "listen to this!"

"Is it recording, Carol?"

"Yes. He's talking about finding a body. Think it's a hoax?"

"I don't know, but we're gonna treat it like it's not."

"Get Don Willard on the phone."

"It's his day off."

"Apologize and tell him to meet us there, you know, the place where the kids hang out. He better take his own car to save time.

Radio Sergeant Vollner and tell him we're meeting at Elm and River Road."

"Should I call the coroner?"

"Not yet. I'll let you know. Oh, and tell those guys not to speed. No lights, either."

They met and walked up Elm Street, which was no more than a narrow, dirt road. According to the phone caller, they'd find a body, out in the open, near the edge of the woods.

"Christ almighty!" shouted Vollner.

"Geez, what a slaughter!" Willard muttered, rubbing the back of his neck.

Chief McCullum stepped around the girl's body, looking down at her. "I was hoping," he said, "that this was a hoax. High School girl, wouldn't you say?" The two others nodded. "I wonder if she's one of ours. Somebody, get something to cover her up." He got on the radio, "Carol, call the coroner and get another officer over here with a spool of yellow tape."

The coroner arrived with a photographer who began setting up his shots.

"Doc, on your way in, did you notice anybody lurking around?" McCullum asked.

"Nope. Well, now, this looks pretty goddam brutal, if you ask me. Wait, what's this?" He squatted down next to her. "She's wearing a ring. Looks like a class ring. 'CHHS'."

"Columbia Hills High School," offered Willard.

"She got her initials on it," Doc continued, "B.B. and 1968."

McCullum got on the radio, again. "Carol, call the Columbia Hills P.D. with this: Female, seventeen, eighteen years old, short, dark hair, tall, athletic build, high school class ring, with initials, 'BB.' Would've been a senior. Get back to me, ASAP."

Waiting only minutes, Carol radioed back. "They've got a match. Her parents phoned in a missing persons, last evening. She is, or *was*, Barbara Lynn Baker."

Hurriedly, putting his shirt and belt back on, he slid into the car. Seeing a pink comb, her comb, on the passenger seat, he gasped, "Oh, shit!" He threw it on the back seat and then decided to wedge it between the seat and the backrest, leaving only a small piece of it showing. "It'll be okay if somebody else finds it."

"All right you guys," McCullum announced, "now comes the fun part. Which one of you wants to come with to tell her parents? Willard, I think you do."

Barbara's mother stared at the officers, for only a moment, before letting out a bone chilling scream and collapsing onto a sofa, sobbing, her hands covering her face. Her husband, head down, turned away, then sat down and held his wife. Both were shaking. Barbara's brothers stayed in their bedrooms until the police left. They had heard everything.

Outside, as they were leaving, "Willard, we're gonna need all the help we can get. Columbia Hills can help us question people and the Sheriff's office …"

"Ed, why? I mean who would do this? What the hell's the motive for killing a kid?"

McCullum, on the phone with Columbia Hills P.D., "Her funeral and burial's gonna be at Elmwood on Monday. Yeah, I know. Why there? I guess somebody donated the plot. Look, it's gonna be private so, I'm putting two uniforms on that detail to keep the curious away. I'd appreciate your help by sending two of yours. You will? Thanks! Monday at noon. By the way, we're not releasing any info to the press 'til she's in the ground."

Early the following Thursday morning. "Chief, I'm getting off shift and I want you to see this before roll call," Vollner said, producing a pink comb. "I found this in the back seat of my squad. I don't have any idea how it got there."

"Lemme, see that. It's a woman's comb. Did you put a woman in the back seat, recently?"

"Not me. Maybe somebody else did."

"I wonder if it could be that girl's comb. I think after roll call, I'll bring it over to her mother's house. Thanks, Vollner."

At roll call, McCullum held up the comb. "Anybody see this comb, before?" The three who were about to go on day watch, shook their heads.

Later, McCullum told his dispatcher that the murdered girl's mother identified the comb as that of her daughter's. It would be entered and joined as evidence, along with the girl's class ring at the Sheriff's office. Exhibits 3 & 4.

"Cheryl, did they actually have the killer in the back seat of a Freemont squad?" Smith asked. "Did the killer intend to keep the comb as a trophy?"

"I don't know what to think, Byron. In all these years, forty-seven of 'em, we're the only ones seriously investigating this case. And the rest of CID are laughing at us, calling us the odd couple."

"Yeah, and the long and the short of it."

"And that I'm babysitting you. Hell, you're only a few years younger than me."

"Worst one I've heard is, the drumstick and the kettle drum."

"Well, Byron, you are a tall, skinny, drinka water and I am short and stocky. They're being poetic."

They both laughed and returned to the discussion of the comb before checking Freemont's squad car logs from August third to August eighth, 1967. The log recorded who drove that particular squad during three shifts.

"Why would a Freemont cop be giving her a ride and having her sit in the back seat? There's no record of her ever being arrested, or even questioned. In fact, she doesn't have a police record in Freemont, or Columbia Hills."

"I was wondering, if she happened to have a boyfriend on the Freemont P.D."

"Maybe she did, Byron, but that still doesn't mean that one of Freemont's finest committed a homicide. He's only guilty of giving her a ride."

"The comb is a key piece of the puzzle, though. There's only one more item in the chain of evidence. It's a long-shot, Cheryl. Her class ring."

"You mean she wasn't buried with it? It wasn't given to her mother?"

"No, we have it."

Smith slid the plastic bag containing the ring, across the conference table to Atkinson. Dried flecks of Barbara Baker's blood remained. It had not undergone DNA analysis, so the detectives asked the lab to test it. They would wait two months for the results.

Smith was the first to get the news from the lab. A female technician phoned, excitement in her voice. "I've got a viable sample! Skin cells embedded in the ring! They are not the victim's!"

"Cheryl!" Smith called across the squad room, "get your stocky ass over here! Never mind, I'll run my skinny ass over there!"

The rest of the detectives stared at both of them and laughed. Smith ignored them and skidded to a stop, just in time, or he would've crashed into her desk. She recoiled, grimacing. He scanned the room, finding his fellow employees still laughing, he frowned and touched the side of his nose with a middle finger.

"Cheryl, conference room."

"What's with you?"

They rushed into the conference room.

"The lab found DNA on the ring."

"So, you're guessing that she must've touched her attacker with her ring?"

"Yes, hit him, or scratched him. She fought back."

"Hold on, Byron. The original suspects got themselves killed. Who's left to do a DNA match? What do we do, try to match hundreds of people?"

"No, we look at who was driving that particular squad, day watch, on August third and fourth. He was also one of three who were first at the crime scene. Chief McCullum noted that Sergeant Herb Vollner found the comb in his squad on the morning of August eighth. Vollner also noted it."

"You're crazy! Freemont cops weren't, aren't that dirty!"

"I think this one was, Cheryl. See, he always drove the same squad, no matter what shift he was working. Sure, other cops drove it, but they didn't find the comb. Vollner did. He must've gotten impatient when nobody else found it."

"How come nobody else found it?"

"I don't know. Maybe it wasn't in plain sight. It doesn't matter. McCullum would've handled it the same way. He didn't realize the significance 'til it was identified by the girl's mother."

"So, you wanna put the finger on Vollner? Do you really think he did it?"

"Look, I found out that Vollner quit the Freemont force, two months later, moved his family down to Southern Minnesota, to Austin, and worked for Austin P.D. for a few years, then quit. For a while, he worked as a security guard at a warehouse before retiring."

"Do you think we should go down there and have a talk with him?"

"Not 'we,' me. I don't want to make him suspicious."

"Are you sure? Byron, it could be dangerous going alone."

"Dangerous? He's seventy-eight years old and living alone…a widower. His kids are grown up and moved away. I'll get his phone number and call ahead."

"Are you gonna tell him about the DNA on the ring?"

"Not right away."

"Should we tell the Captain what you're up to?"

"No. Leave Crowley out of this 'til I'm absolutely sure."

Smith called Vollner and let the phone ring several times before he answered. Smith introduced himself and explained why he was calling.

"You haven't cracked that case yet? Vollner rasped, "It's decades old, for god's sake! And why are you asking me?"

"Because," Smith answered, "you're the last survivor of the original cops who were the first on the crime scene."

"I know that McCullum wouldn't be alive, 'cause he was older, but what about Willard?"

"Nope. He's dead, too. A few years ago. So, if you're gonna be home in the next couple of days, I'd like to come down and talk to you about it, Mr. Vollner. We could meet anyplace you want."

"Where could I go? I'm a fuckin' cripple in a wheelchair. I don't go anyplace, anymore."

"Well, could I come to your home?"

Reluctantly, Vollner said, "If you think it'll help, sure. But, I tell ya, you're way out in left field."

"I'll call you when I get to Austin."

"It's all set, Cheryl, I'm going to Austin to see Vollner."

"You're sure about this, then? Are you gonna have the Austin P.D. standing by?"

"No. None of that. I'm gonna begin by treating him as a non-suspect."

"At least you'll have a nice drive…seeing all the fall colors…the reds, the golds, the yellows…"

"Yeah, decomposing leaves."

"Well, aren't you the cynical one. Are you gonna take one of your girlfriends with you?"

"No."

"All business, Byron. That's my boy. I guess cops weren't meant to have a life. You start out with shift-work and hard cases … spouses and friends don't understand our work. I got divorced because of it. My advice is to stay single 'til you retire."

"I intend to."

"There are some advantages though. For instance, I've got two teenage daughters, you know, and when their dates come over, the first thing I tell them, is that I'm a cop. So, if they're harboring any bad intentions, they run away. My girls hate it, but too bad, so sad."

"Crowley told me I could have four vacation days," Smith told Atkinson. "I'll stay in a motel in Austin and I'll call you as soon as I check-in."

Atkinson smiled wanly and said, "I want you to call me the whole time you're down there, understand? I'm the only one who knows why you're going."

"Yeah, it's a wild goose chase based on a hunch."

Atkinson's smile faded. She said, "Suppose you happen to be right about Vollner, how're you going to prove it? Do you think he's gonna volunteer a DNA sample?"

"Maybe if he's innocent, he will. If he acts, in any way, guilty, I'll come back with a couple of Austin cops."

A whole goddam week, thought Vollner, *and nobody found the comb. I'll just tell McCullum that I saw something pink wedged in the backseat of my squad, and pulled it out, surprised that it turned out to be a big comb. I'm sure he'll question me about it and, of course, I won't know a thing.*

Smith didn't think that Austin was that busy of a place, but he decided to make a reservation anyway, at the *Holiday Inn*; familiar surroundings no matter where one traveled.

It was a one hundred thirty-mile trip. He took the less than scenic I-35 route nearly straight South, almost to Albert Lea, turning East on I-90 and continuing on a mercifully shorter distance to Austin, Minnesota. Smith found the Oakland Place exit and took it to 5th Avenue and then, on to 19th Street. Vollner lived close to the hotel.

On the way, he noticed a murder of crows perched high in a pine tree watching him as he slowed, nearing the city. A thin smile crossed his lips. Was it a coincidence that he was investigating a murder? No, Smith didn't believe, never believed, in coincidences.

Checking into the hotel, his first call was to his partner, Atkinson, telling her that he had safely arrived. The next call was to Vollner, setting an appointment, at his home, for the following morning.

After he'd unpacked, Smith drove over to 5th Avenue to preview Vollner's house. It was a small bungalow, perhaps a two-bedroom, almost like the kind in which Barbara Baker had lived.

As he had studied the case for the past three years, it occurred to Smith that Baker's murder was similar to Poe's, *The Mystery of Marie Roget,* based on the true, brutal, 1841 slaying of Mary Cecilia Rogers. He also concluded that both stories, fact and fiction, were analogous to the Baker case.

Even though Sergeant Herb Vollner was not involved in the investigation of the murder of Barbara Lynn Baker, he asked to see the case file, which included the autopsy report. He became horrified at its findings. His intended red herring of a sexual assault, by removing her shorts and underwear, didn't work. But, the most terrifying thing to Vollner, was that she was not pregnant. *She had told him that she was pregnant with his child. My god!* Vollner thought, *she didn't have to die! On the other hand, she tried to use blackmail.*

Smith found it hard to relax by watching TV in his room; he was thinking about how to approach Vollner with pertinent questions. Innocent people usually don't remember where they were or, what they were doing a week ago, much less, over forty years ago. The guilty always seem to know. *Would Vollner know exactly where he was on the afternoon of August third, 1967? Where would Vollner say he was? Would saying that he was across town, be his alibi?* Smith wondered. *The City of Freemont is almost eleven square miles. Would he say that he was patrolling within his assigned grid? Or, home for lunch?*

Smith knew precisely how to question suspects and Vollner had no idea that the Andrews County Crime Lab had found DNA, perhaps his, on Baker's high school class ring.

As Smith got out of his car, his cellphone rang.

"It's me, Cheryl. I've got a fantastic idea."

"Not now. I'm at Vollner's house … Almost at the door."

"Listen, leave your phone open. On speaker. That way, everything he says can be recorded and he'll be none the wiser."

"Okay. You're a good Mom."

"Shut up, Byron."

Smith knocked once.

"Come in," Vollner shouted, "it's unlocked."

"Mr. Vollner? I'm …"

"I know who you are."

"This seems to be a nice, quiet neighborhood, Mr. Vollner."

"Yeah. People gone to work and kids in school."

"I didn't see a ramp out in front," Smith said, observing Vollner's wheelchair.

"There's one out in back," replied Vollner, "more shade back there. Geez, they grow you guys big, these days. I'm getting a crick in my neck looking up at you."

Smith looked down the hallway to his left and saw a bathroom at the end of the hall, flanked by two bedrooms on opposite sides, the doors open. He stood in a small living room, furnished with an overstuffed armchair, a lampstand by its side and a three-cushioned sofa. The kitchen was directly in front of him.

"Where's your TV?"

"I use one of the bedrooms for a library and a TV room. Let's sit at the table," Vollner motioned with his thumb. "Pull the chair away. I'll just sit in this goddam thing."

There was nothing in Vollner's face, thought Smith, *not his voice, either. Deadpan, blunted affect.*

Behind wire-rimmed glasses, Vollner's dark, hooded eyes looked like bottomless wells, revealing absolutely nothing; neither apprehension, nor guile, nor guilt, nor innocence. He held a folded newspaper in his lap.

Smith matched Vollner's countenance as he held out his hand to shake Vollner's thin, white hand, mapped with blue veins and smooth to the touch.

Of course his hand was smooth, cops never did manual labor. Then, Smith became aware of his own thinning blond hair, when Vollner, at his age, had thick hair, the color of steel wool, which had only slightly receded. But, the photos that Smith had seen of him as a younger man on Freemont's police force, depicted a large, broad-shouldered man. The older Vollner looked nearly skeletal. His shoulders now, had narrowed.

As if to explain his appearance and his being imprisoned in a wheelchair, Vollner uttered, "Bad hips. Knees are shot." Changing the subject, Vollner asked, "Place looks pretty good, don't it?"

Smith nodded.

"I got a woman who comes in and cleans twice a week. Not only that, she does my laundry and cooks, too. She freezes food for me to have on days she's not here. It pisses her off whenever she sees an empty pizza box in the trash. After my wife died, I thought that

I could live alone. This place turned into a regular dump. My wife kept me from being a pig for fifty-three years."

They moved toward the yellow, Formica-topped, kitchen table which sat against the wall, under a wide window with green nylon curtains, pulled back.

"Want some coffee? Just made it."

"Thanks, don't mind if I do," Smith answered.

"Got sugar and milk. No cream."

"That's okay. I drink it black."

"Help yourself. Grab two cups out of the cupboard."

Smith placed a steaming cup in front of Vollner and took a seat opposite him. Both men would henceforth try to maintain uninterrupted eye contact.

"Okay, I'm ready. Let the interrogation begin," Vollner stated, dramatically, but without the flair.

"It's not an interrogation. It's only an interview."

"Well then, let's get it over with, Lieutenant."

"I explained, on the phone, that you were one of the first to arrive on the murder scene and then, there's the matter of the girl's comb that you found in the backseat of your squad car…"

"A lot of cops drove that car and we, any of us, would've *seen* that fuckin' comb sticking out of a pocket, when we search somebody, before we put them in the back."

"Did you ever hear of any cop letting someone ride back there who wasn't searched?"

"No. Never. We were discouraged, but if we ever had any casual passengers, they'd ride in front."

"So, Barbara Baker would never have ridden in the back of yours, or any other Freemont squad?"

"If she had, she would've ridden in the front. A suspect always rides in the back."

"It's possible, then, that she was riding in that particular car?"

"Sure. Let's say that she was hitchhiking from somewhere in Freemont to Columbia Hills. A cop picked her up, lectured her about the dangers of hitchhiking and drove her home."

"That makes sense. Was she in your car?"

"I didn't know that kid. Never saw her … alive, that is. I didn't know any Columbia Hills kids."

"Did you help question people in Columbia Hills who might've known Barbara?"

"No."

"Recently, my partner and I re-interviewed people who knew her. They all said that she was an 'unlikely victim.'"

"Yeah, I read the reports and that's what everybody said, back in '67. So, is that all you got? Is that it?"

"Not quite. We'll keep working to solve this, especially to give the girl's mother some, as much as I hate the word, 'closure'. She's in her eighties and in poor health, so …"

"Is her father alive?"

"No, he died in '72. Her three brothers are still around. We think they need closure, too."

"How're you gonna end this when you don't even know how her comb got into the backseat of a police car?"

"I want you to stay, Sgt. Vollner, but if you think things might work better for you somewhere else, then I've got to let you go, even though it's not a good time with that girl's murder, only two months ago. Where are you going?"

"I already checked into it. There's an opening in Austin." *Anywhere,* Vollner thought to himself, *is better than hanging around here, maybe being scrutinized as a suspect. Got to go as far away as I can.*

"Okay, then. Turn in your uniform, badge and service revolver."

"Thanks, Chief, I mean, Ed."

"We think the comb was planted in the backseat and for a while, we thought the comb was important. But, her class ring …"

"Her class ring?"

"Yes, it has someone's DNA, besides hers, on it. Do you know about DNA?"

"Yeah, everybody does. I like to watch those cold case shows where DNA evidence solves old crimes. Whose DNA is on her ring?"

"We don't know yet, but we must've tested fifty people, so far," Smith lied. "You know as well as I do, that when you have multiple suspects, you begin a process of elimination."

"Sure, I know. Everybody starts out as a suspect."

There he sits, thought Smith, *cool as a cucumber, even though he's a suspect, the only one, at this point.*

"We believe that the DNA on the ring could belong to her killer."

At the first sign of agitation, Vollner placed his newspaper on the table and began fingering the edges. His jaw muscles flexed.

"How do you know the DNA was the killer's?"

"Well, we're still not positive, but there were some skin cells on it like she scratched, or cut her attacker. All the people we gathered samples from, were anxious to prove their innocence."

"Don't you think she might've scratched somebody else accidently?"

"Oh, sure. Her mother said she never took that ring off. So, we're exploring every possibility."

"Lieutenant, do you have a point to make, or did you come all the way down here to bounce your theories off me?"

Smith was getting tired of fencing with Vollner. He was being too careful with his questions. It was time to get what he'd come for.

"I want you to know that I checked your military record and your record with Freemont, including your shorter stint with Austin P.D. All exemplary. Not one black mark."

"So what?" Could you please get to the point? I'm not getting any younger."

"Codis matches up DNA ..."

"Yeah, yeah, yeah. I know all about that. DNA helps prove innocence, or his guilt."

Smith kept his voice a steady, unemotional monotone. "You know, since I've been working this case and I've seen pictures in

34

her yearbook, of a smiling, teenage girl ... well, I can imagine her as she was; someone young enough to be a middle-aged couple's daughter and now, if she would've lived, she'd be old enough to be someone's grandmother."

Smith noticed that Vollner, after he had been slumping in his wheelchair, was now sitting more erect. He also began to wonder why he could only see the man's right hand fiddling with the newspaper, while his left, as far as Smith could tell, continued to rest on his lap. *That doesn't mean anything,* he assured himself.

"You could prove your innocence by giving me a DNA sample ... voluntarily, of course."

"Yeah. What kind?"

Suddenly, Vollner threw the newspaper off the table. Smith, surprised, diverted his attention away from Vollner. The moment the paper hit the floor, Vollner, with his left hand, raised and pointed a .22 semi-automatic at Smith's head and squeezed the trigger.

A small, dark hole appeared in Smith's forehead. His body stiffened and his head snapped back, then lolled toward his left shoulder, before his momentum pitched him forward, his head crashed, slammed onto the table top. Smith's coffee cup shattered under his chest. A rivulet of blood trickled from his wound.

Vollner wheeled over to Smith and pulled on a pair of glove liners that he had on his lap, along with his gun.

There, under his sport coat, on his belt, was a holstered 9mm. Vollner withdrew it and lifted Smith's limp arm, placed the weapon in the lifeless hand a fired off three rounds, one into the wall and two into the cupboard behind where Vollner had been sitting. He let Smith's gun drop to the floor. Then, he went to the closet to replace the glove liners into their leather shells. According to his well-thought out plan, Vollner phoned the Austin police.

Pretending to be out of breath, he explained that a cop, a detective, shot at him and that he, in turn, shot back and killed him in self-defense. *They'd buy that,* thought Vollner, *sure they would. The younger man tried to kill a poor, old cripple.*

Within a few minutes, Vollner began to hear sirens. Three squads and one unmarked pulled up at the curb, in front of his house. He started toward the door, but changed his mind, returned to his spot at the table and assumed a demeanor of extreme shock. He raised his arms as officers entered the house, guns drawn.

"I'm Herb Vollner. I'm a retired Austin cop." He put his arms down when one of the uniformed cops picked up the .22, then the 9-mm and released the clips. "I always keep it loaded," Vollner explained.

He saw another uniform whisper something to a man in a gray suit. The man introduced himself to Vollner as Detective Sergeant Singleton. Cocking his thumb toward Smith's remains. "Was he here on business? Investigative business?"

"I really don't know. There was a murder in Freemont, where I was a cop. That was years and years ago. Well, the case recently became active and he came here asking me all kinds of questions."

"Yeah? What kind of questions?"

"Oh, things like, 'did I know the victim?' 'Did I have any idea who did it?'"

"Why did he shoot at you?" and added, incredulously, "How could he miss you three times at close range?"

"I bent over to pick up my newspaper just when he started firing," Vollner shrugged. "You know cops are notoriously bad shots."

"Obviously, you're not. Hey," the detective asked the others, "did anybody call the M.E.?"

"They're on their way," someone answered.

"We'll stay 'til they remove the body," the detective said, blocking Vollner's view of Smith.

The Medical Examiner arrived with two EMTs who maneuvered a gurney through the front door.

"You're in luck," Singleton told the M.E., "no brains to scrape off the wall. Small caliber." The M.E. laughed politely.

The EMTs loaded Smith onto the gurney. "Anything else, detective?"

"Yeah, take his cell phone out. I think it's in his shirt pocket."

They covered Smith's body, strapped it down and left.

"Guess what?" Singleton waved the cell phone in front of Vollner. "A funny thing happened just before you called us."

Vollner tensed, his hands gripped the arms of his wheelchair.

"We got a phone call from a Lt. Cheryl Atkinson up in Andrews County. She was Smith's partner. They kept an open line on this cell."

"What the hell you driving at?" Vollner's face paled.

"She told us that there was a single shot and about thirty seconds later, three shots. Thirty seconds later, Vollner! Gentlemen," he instructed a couple of beefy officers, "stand him up and cuff him. Read him his rights. Herbert Vollner, you are under arrest for the murder of Lieutenant Byron Smith. First degree murder.

"We'll hold you in the Mower County Jail overnight. In the morning, deputies from Andrews County'll take you into custody. There's something I can't figure out."

Vollner mumbled something incoherently.

"You killed a guy because he asked you for your DNA. You were that afraid it would connect you to that girl's murder in 1967. Did it ever occur to you that it wouldn't be your DNA? Or, that it'd be inconclusive? Or, how 'bout this one, Smith could've been bluffing."

Vollner, his head hanging, said nothing.

"At any rate, they won't ask, they'll take your DNA and if it's a match, you'll probably serve two consecutive life sentences. Look on the bright side, Vollner, you'll never have to face a parole board. Wheel his ass outta here."

eaching the outskirts of Saint Cloud, Minnesota, I started driving eastbound on State Highway 10 and quickly accelerated, leveling off at sixty miles per hour. It was late summer 1975. Excluding intermittent stops, I figured to reach Minneapolis by early afternoon. A few miles later, my life was about to change. That's when I met her. I had stopped at a truck stop. A tall, young woman, in her early twenties sidled up to me as I was paying for my coffee and cinnamon roll, at the cash register.

"How far are you going?" she asked.

"To Minneapolis."

I didn't look at her right away, but when I did, I was surprised at how tall she was. I'm not a tall man, but she had to be four inches taller than I. She had short, straight, black hair ... almost too black for her light complexion. She wore a man's white shirt, with the collar turned up and baggy blue jeans. The only things she wore that were remotely feminine were large, hoop earrings. Nonetheless, I found myself strangely attracted to her.

I turned to walk out the door and there she was, tagging along at my side. I stopped when we were outside and waited for her to say something.

"Look," she sighed, "I'm tired of hitchhiking. I just need a ride and it would be perfectly lovely if you're going as far as Minneapolis. My aunt and uncle live there and I want to visit for a while before fall semester."

"Where do you go to school?" I asked.

"Saint Cloud. Majoring in Religion."

That's just great. That's so very great. However, if I play my cards right, that's not going to matter.

"Yeah? I go to Saint Cloud too. Only I'm majoring in History ... going home to visit my folks."

She picked up a small suitcase that was standing at her feet, which I hadn't noticed before.

"Don't you think we should get going? By the way, my name's Jessica, Jess for short, what's yours?"

"It's John."

"Yes ... John, one of the Apostles."

Jess opened the car door and tossed her suitcase onto the backseat and sank, breathlessly, into the passenger seat.

"This is a nice, large car. What kind is it? Is it new?"

"It's a Ford and it's a few years old."

She was looking out the window, when I looked over and asked, jokingly, "Don't you really know what make of car this is? You're not from around here, are you?"

Jess threw her head back and laughed.

She put her left knee on the seat and draped her arm over the back, facing me. I caught a whiff of lilac sachet powder which struck me as a little odd for a girl in her twenties. It was something my grandma would've worn. *I really don't need to be thinking about Grandma, right now.*

"Where abouts in Minneapolis are you going, Jess?"

"Northeast."

"Great, so am I. So, do you make this hitchhiking trip often?"

"Yes, usually between semesters. You know, it never fails to amaze me ... I mean the brazen effrontery of some men. Just because I'm hitchhiking, doesn't mean that I want anything else, other than a ride."

"Yeah, Jess, it can be pretty bad, sometimes."

"Pretty bad? Recently, there was a man who would've driven me all the way to Corpus Christi, if I had asked him. He was completely horrid!"

With that comment, Jess glanced at me, smirked, then broke into a wide, beautiful smile, revealing a perfect row of white teeth in a dazzling display of periodontal pulchritude.

"Do you mind if I take my boots off?"

"No," I said, "you go right ahead."

She loosened the rawhide laces and pulled the tan, leather, hiking boots off. I was looking at her hair, when I noticed her eyes. They were icy blue, which belied the color of her hair, as well as her complexion. I wondered if it was dyed.

"John, do you mind rolling up the window? I've been standing outside most of the morning and I'm getting a chill."

I cranked up the window as fast as I could.

"So, Jess, how much longer do you have to go to school?"

"I graduate this coming spring. Then, I plan to attend the University of Minnesota for my Master's. What about you, John?"

"I'm starting my sophomore year."

"John, my dear, you're older than I and you're only a sophomore? How come it's taking you so long?"

"Because of the war, Jess. I was drafted into the Army."

"Oh, yes, the war. It's begun by old men for young men to fight."

"Exactly. I think Korea and Vietnam were only continuations of World War Two."

"John, you could go back to World War One to support that theory."

"Yeah, that's right. Back to 1917."

"I don't know whether you're obtuse, or whether you're just being ethnocentric, but that War began in Europe, in 1914. Are you sure that you're a History major?"

"Oh yeah, I forgot."

I looked over at Jess to find that she was staring at me, expressionless. "Regarding Vietnam," she spoke, then paused, "President Nixon was at the center of the entire matter, wasn't he?"

"Certainly," I said, "besides the War, there was Watergate and the Pentagon Papers embroilment. But, look on the bright side; he'll never have anything named after him, no streets, no schools, nothing. That'll be his place in history."

"Oh, the poor, Machiavellian man!" she commented, sarcastically.

Checking the gas gauge, I turned toward Jess, who was looking straight ahead. *What a great profile,* I thought, *absolutely perfect!*

"Jess, we'd better stop in Princeton for gas. While we're there, we could find a café and get some lunch."

She looked at me and smiled, "That would be simply divine. I'm completely famished."

Simply divine? Famished? Who'd she think she was, Katherine Hepburn?

We saw an inviting place on the town's main street. A sign hung over the sidewalk which read, simply, "CAFÉ." There was another sign in the window that said, "GOOD FOOD." Whenever I saw a sign like that, I've always wondered if the owner thought it rhymed.

The large, plate-glass windows were filmy ... opaque ... probably from decades of grease and cigarette smoke. We went in. A bell tinkled above the door.

A beefy cop, sitting on a stool at the counter, turned and stared at us, then turned back to his coffee. An elderly couple, sitting in a corner booth, holding hands across their table, didn't notice us at first, then looked at us and sadly nodded their heads.

"Just ignore them," Jess whispered, "let's sit over here."

A tall, gaunt man with shoulder-length, dirty, gray hair, came out from behind the counter, walked over to our booth and asked us what we wanted. We both ordered black coffee and before I could look at the menu, Jess suggested ham and eggs. I agreed and thought that maybe, over a meal and coffee, I could get to know her better.

She took a sip of coffee and said, while gazing out the window, absent-mindedly, "You might be the one, John."

"What? The one?" I asked. *Yes, I am the one,* I thought. *One what? Who the hell cares!* "Jess, what do you mean, I'm the one?" I leaned toward her.

"I said that you might be!" She dropped her hands on the table and leaned back, her face pink with anger. "Besides, I was only thinking aloud."

I made her angry for some reason. God, don't make her angry! "It's okay, Jess. No need to explain."

She sat there, with a faint, enigmatic smile on her lips and stared wistfully, out the window.

Fine, let her be a riddle, if she wants. My greatest fear, however, was that what began so amicably, would end on a sour note.

When we finished eating and were having our second cup of coffee, Jess said, abruptly, "We'd better be leaving now. Oh, and thank you, John, for lunch."

We headed back to Highway 10, which had changed to a four-lane, indicating that we were getting closer to the larger suburbs of Minneapolis.

"What's the next town, John?"

"Elk River, I think. Yes, Elk River."

"This is a dreadfully long ride, isn't it?"

"Not when you're in the company of someone like you, Jess."

Neither Jess nor I said another word, until we took the southbound exit onto University Avenue from I-694.

"We're almost there now. Where exactly, do you want me to let you out?"

"I'll let you know."

We traveled along University and soon saw the Minneapolis skyline a few miles ahead.

"We're right in the heart of Northeast, Jess. Just tell me where you want to get out. I can go further than where I'm going."

"I'm sure you can, John. It should be coming up, soon. Oh, here we are. You may let me out at the next corner."

"You want to get out on Thirteenth?"

"Yes, John, and by the way, I found your company quite marvelous."

I pulled to the curb a few feet in front of the semaphore. She grabbed her suitcase, waited a few seconds for the light to change and flounced, in front of my car, across University. Lyrics to the song, "The Gal That Got Away," crooned by Sinatra, in his best post-Ava Gardner period, flashed through my brain. Frank may have let Ava get away, but I wasn't about to let Jess get away that easily.

I leaped from the car and looked east on Thirteenth. I didn't think she went into the bar on the corner, or the Ritz Theater. Maybe she ducked into a building in between. I found myself standing in front of the Hellenic Café. I tried to enter, but the door was locked. Just then, a young Latino, carrying a push broom, came scurrying over. "Sir, we're not open yet," he yelled through the glass door.

"Did you let a dark-haired woman in here?"

The young man unlocked the door and motioned me inside. "Did you see her?" I asked again.

"No, I didn't see anybody." He locked the door behind me. "Are you hungry, sir?" The cook should be here in a few minutes.

"No thanks. I don't really care for Greek food."

"This is not a Greek restaurant. Oh, the name of the place confused you. The owner's wife's name is Helen."

His answer satisfied my query until I saw a large, framed photograph of the Parthenon hanging above the wooden booths and across the room, bolted to the wall, an iron cross with four equal arms at right angles. *A Greek cross*, I thought, *why would this kid lie to me?*

"All right, I guess I'd better get going. You can unlock the door, now." The boy dug into his pocket and pulled out a ring of keys.

What's the use. I'll probably never see her again. I got into my car and drove to the nearby Mac and Cap's for a couple of bumps.

Mac and Cap's was not only known for its giant football on the roof, it was also known for the black and white framed photos of Minnesota amateur and professional sports heroes. The photos seemed to cover every square inch of wall space.

I sat at the bar and ordered a Windsor on-the-rocks. I could see the photos in the reflection of the bar mirror and swiveled around to get a closer look. Wearing a football jersey, was the portrait of Ernie Nevers. Below it, was an inscribed brass plaque, which read: "ERNIE NEVERS—Willow River, MN—Duluth Eskimos and Chicago Cardinals." The picture right next to it, nearly made my heart stop. It looked exactly like Jess! "Okay," I whispered, "what the hell's going on here? If I were losing my mind, wouldn't I be the first to know?" "No," I answered myself, "I'd be the last to know."

I squinted and read the plaque: "JESSICA WEBB—Saint Cloud, MN—1932 Olympics—Los Angeles—Track and Field." *No, it's gotta be a coincidence. It just can't be! 1932? She'd be in her sixties!*

Stunned, I turned back to the bartender and asked if he'd heard of her.

"Oh, sure, I knew her. She's a local legend. Moved to Northeast right after the Olympics. Did you know her, too?"

"Yeah, at least *I* think so. I gave her a ride from Saint Cloud, today."

"Liar! That's impossible!" his voice cracked, "she died a few months ago."

"Did she have a daughter?" I asked nervously.

"As a matter of fact, she did."

My relief was short-lived, as he added, "She never married, but she adopted a daughter; a little Korean girl."

I caught a glimpse of my somber, slack-jawed reflection in the mirror. I looked like a guy who could sit there and drink triples, steadily, for a couple of hours.

herapy

o you know why you're here, Jason?"

"Sure, it's because people think I'm nuts."

"What do you think is the *real* reason?"

Why is she asking me questions, when she already knows the answers? Mom had set up the appointment, so they must've talked about why they thought I need therapy.

She stares at me and waits patiently for an answer. I take my time and look around the room. There's a cherry-wood coffee table between us, the same color desk, and above her orderly, nearly bare desk, hangs her framed diploma: A MASTER'S DEGREE IN SOCIAL WORK HAS BEEN CONFERRED UPON GEORGIA ANN MOORE. This creature has a name. And she's not bad looking.

I lean against the arm of the tan, three-cushioned, leather sofa, which matches the chair she's sitting on.

"My family, especially my mom, thinks I'm delusional." I smirk with the satisfaction that I used the right word. She begins scratching notes, with a pencil, on a yellow legal pad.

"Does your father think that, as well?" she says without looking up.

"Maybe. I don't know. My mother's the one who's pushy."

"Yes, perhaps she is. She said that you think you're a werewolf."

"Think?" I feel anger mounting. "Think? I know I am! It's real! Don't you believe me?"

"I believe that you believe it's real."

It sounds like a canned statement. She looks at me, crosses her legs and tugs at the hem of her blue, denim jumper to cover an exposed knee and goes back to scribbling her notes. While she has her head down, it gives me the opportunity to study her. Under the jumper, she's wearing a white t-shirt. Not the underwear kind. Perched on the top of her head is a pair of black-rimmed glasses. Her hair is light-brown with blond highlights.

She looks up with pale, blue eyes framed with black eyeliner and mascara, the only evidence that I can see, of makeup. Her nose is nicely shaped, thin and it turns up slightly at the end. I notice that her lips are full, without lipstick and naturally pink. She's wearing white tennis shoes with blue anklets. I hate it when women wear loose-fitting jumpers, because it hides everything. But, she's dressed exactly the way I'd imagine a social worker to dress.

"So, how did you become a werewolf?" she gets right to the point.

I tell her that a couple of years ago, my parents, my little sister and I were camping in a tent. It was a fairly nice campground flanked by some woods of pine trees and oaks. We were sitting in lawn chairs, facing a campfire while my dad was hatching up ghost stories. He probably thought that it was the only thing to do in front of a campfire. A full moon was large and golden, beginning its ascent into a black sky, studded with a million stars, which could never been seen in the city. My mom and sister pretended that they hadn't heard the stories before, but I was bored and decided to walk into the woods. Besides, I had to take a leak. I stopped at the nearest tree. When I was done, I heard heavy breathing behind me. I zipped up my jeans and spun around. A huge wolf, it must've been seven feet tall, stood on her hind legs, teeth bared and growling. I, like, turned to run away, but she lunged at me, grabbed my arm and sunk her scissor-sharp teeth deep into my flesh. I struggled to pull away, then she let go and ran deeper into the woods.

"Why did you say, 'she?' How did you know that the wolf was a she?"

"She told me."

"She could talk?"

"No, she like, communicated it telepathically. She also told me that she was a werewolf and that I would become one, too."

"Then what happened?" Georgia Ann Moore asks, as she runs the pencil eraser down her jawline and taps it on her chin. Her eyes widen, her eyebrows rise and three distinct furrows appear on her forehead; a look of concern that she probably practiced over and over in front of a mirror 'til she was certain it looked convincing.

I go on with my story: As I ran, I cradled my forearm with my other hand. The blood gushed between my fingers. The wound was so painful that I thought I'd pass out. I looked to see the damage. I saw that she bit through the muscle and thought that I could see bone.

As soon as I could see the tent and the campfire, I started yelling for help. My mom ran to meet me. My dad leaned on his cane, slow to get up.

"What the hell's the matter?" she screamed.

I held my arm out in front of me, "Look, look at this!"

"Look at what? I don't see anything!" she rolled her eyes. Dad and Sis ambled over and stared. I looked at what should have been a mangled arm and what should have been blood spattered on my clothes, but there was nothing. Then I made the mistake of telling them about the werewolf. Mom and Sis huffed dismissively and walked away and Dad said that I was trying to top him with a better spook story.

Georgia leaned back in her chair. "That was very interesting. Well, I guess our time is up. See you next Monday at 4, then?"

"Yeah."

My afternoon appointments were the last of her day. I figured that she wouldn't be as burned out as she would be on a Friday.

The wolf issue isn't even discussed during the second session. She wants to know about my family dynamic. What is our relationship with each other? How well, if at all, do we get along?

She begins her usual prodding concerning my parents. She's wearing another jumper. It's navy blue with a powder blue, long-sleeved blouse and open-toed sandals.

"Do your parents have a lot of arguments? Have you witnessed some of them?"

"Yeah."

"Can you elaborate?"

"Sure. When I don't see the fights, I sometimes hear them. My mom usually starts the argument … she always seems to be pissed off about something. Excuse me, angry."

"That's okay. Please go on. What is she angry about?"

"Well, my dad was in Desert Storm. He stepped on a land mine and blew his left leg off, from the knee down."

With that well-practiced look of mixed concern and sympathy, she leans forward and announces, "How awful!"

"He, like, limps around on a prosthetic and a cane. He got his old job back, but he can only work part-time. My mom had to go back to work to make ends meet. I don't know what she has to bitch about. He gets a disability check from the VA every month. But, she yells at him all the time. He says a couple of words back and turns around and walks away like a whipped, three-legged dog."

"And how do you feel about that?"

"How do I feel? I think it's a pretty horseshit thing for her to do."

"Can you describe your relationship with your sister?"

"She's twelve. What can I say? I think she's from another planet," I laugh and she smiles. "Actually, we do our best to ignore each other."

"You have nothing in common?"

"Nothing. Jordan's an exact duplicate of my mom."

"Would you say that you get along with your dad, better?"

"A little bit, but any man who allows himself to be pushed around like that, doesn't have my respect."

"Do you think he respects you?"

"What the hell has any of this gotta do with lycanthropy?" I don't mean to say it, but there it is, hovering over this room. I look up at her and cough into my fist.

She stares at me and all she says is, "It may have a lot of significance, Jason."

By the third session, I was becoming familiar enough to the security guard, who was posted at a small desk in the lobby that he's let me walk by without checking in with him. "Mel," that's what his plastic nameplate read, had little to say to me and I tried not to even acknowledge him.

The noisy sounds of his huffing and puffing were hard to ignore. If I looked at him, his dark, dead eyes would follow me. *Big, fat, ugly, old bastard,* I thought, every time I walked past him.

I don't know what to call my therapist. Miss Moore? Mrs. Moore? She doesn't wear any wedding ring. I think I'll try calling her, Miss Moore and see what she says. Georgia's younger than my mom and ten times, maybe a hundred times prettier.

Her office is on the main floor of the three-story "Professional Building." She was probably afraid that if her office was on the top floor, her clients might jump out the window.

"Hello, Jason," she greets me with a smile. She's wearing, yet another goddam jumper. This one's tan and I try to put the image of a closet full of jumpers out of my mind.

"Hi, Miss Moore," I say, looking for a reaction. She flashes me a stunned look like I've invaded her privacy, which I think is okay since she's invaded mine.

"Yes, I guess you may call me, 'Miss.'" she says abruptly, with a wave of her hand. "Are we ready to get started?"

I smile, thinking that I've hit a nerve. "Yes."

"How's school and your job going, Jason?"

She knows about my part-time job at the supermarket, stocking shelves and that I'm a part-time student at the community college. I never told her that I flunked the entrance exam at the university. I lied when I said that I just "wanted to get my generals out of the way" at the community college.

"It's fine at school, but my job is stupid and boring."

"Do you like college?"

"It's just fine," I reiterate.

"Let's talk about something else then," she nods. "How about your relationships with your friends?"

"I did have some friends, mostly girlfriends, but I don't have any, what you'd call, 'friends.'"

"Mostly girlfriends? Well, then, tell me about them."

"There was this doughnut shop, where I used to hang out, the first summer after I graduated high school. All the girls who worked there, looked pretty hot and I dated all of them, except for

51

the married chick. Her husband came in to check on her one night and, like, gave me a dirty look."

Georgia laughs, "Did he think you were hitting on her?"

"Maybe he thought that, but I wasn't."

"So, you said that you had dated all the rest of the girls. Did you feel that this was some sort of, shall we say, conquest?"

"No!" I emphatically say, raising my voice. "I liked them. Even the bitchy blond who was probably jealous, because I paid more attention to the brunettes."

"You like girls and women with the exception of the 'bitchy blond.' Any other exceptions?"

Probing and prodding. Is this all she's going to do in this session?

"If you're talking about my mom, I'd have to include her, too." I realize that she's obviously trying to make some kind of connection, so I say what she wants to hear.

"Jason, that's very intuitive of you." She sounds as if she's accomplished something and she says exactly what I expect her to say.

The fourth session, which she would later say was the most productive and that I really opened up, was probably for me the most exciting one. She greets me at the door. This time, she's wearing her glasses on her face and not on her head. The black frames make her look like an owl. I find a reason to celebrate; she's not wearing a jumper. She looks exhausted, for some reason and walks ahead of me to her chair. She's wearing a shiny, black pair of pants, which are tight around her hips and butt. I watch her ass as she approaches her chair. She's got the ass of a grown woman, not the chicken butt of a teenager. Her blouse is white, long-sleeved, with thin, vertical, purple stripes.

The more I study her, the more my dick starts to move around. I've always realized that it's got a mind of its own. But, I feel that I'm more in control of it now. When I was in the sixth grade, I'd get a hard-on for no reason at all. I'd look out the classroom window and see a squirrel scampering up a tree and I'd get a hard-on. One day, my teacher asked the class about state capitals. She asked, "What is the capital of California?" A few hands shot up.

She had the habit of calling on kids who didn't have their hands raised. I didn't raise my hand because of my bone. Of course, she called on me. If a kid knew the answer, they had to stand up and deliver. I memorized the capitol of every state, but I said, "I don't know, teacher." The answer was Sacramento, but I didn't want anybody to see my stiffy, especially the girls. Now, of course, I don't mind if any girl sees it.

My therapist drops into her chair. "Is anything the matter, Miss Moore?"

"No. Why do you ask?"

"Oh, I don't know. Just interested. So, how come you're not married?"

She looks away, then turns to look at me and flips a page over on her notes. Her eyes narrow, her lips are pursed. She leans forward. I sense anger, but then her face softens.

"Aren't we here to discuss your issues, Jason? We're not here to discuss mine."

Maybe I was the one who was making a breakthrough. Her issues? She had issues? How the hell could her issues be compared to mine? She's probably not married and I'm definitely a werewolf. I don't get it. Maybe if I pounced on her and tore her to shreds, she might think that my issues were more important than hers.

"Let's see now, last week you were talking about girls at the doughnut shop and that you dated most of them. How do you think those dates went?"

"Pretty good. I'd take them to a movie, or dinner at a nice restaurant. Not both because it would've been too expensive."

"And what was your purpose of going out on dates with these girls?"

I laugh, "What do you think?" Then I'm kind of embarrassed at what she must be thinking.

She smiles broadly, showing all of her brilliantly, white teeth. "Was it to have sex with as many of them as possible?"

I know that's what she's driving at. I pretend that I'm shocked at her question and bury my face in my hands. I look through spread fingers and see that she's still staring at me in that same, passive way. She moves her glasses to the top of her head, leans forward, smiling, waiting for my answer. I cross my legs to hide my full-fledged boner.

"No. There was only one that I really wanted to have sex with. She was different than the rest of 'em. Even though she was the same age, she seemed older and smarter."

"Would you say, more poised?"

"Yeah, more poised and she was hot, besides!"

"So, what happened with her?"

"Well, she was, like, telling me about this kid that she was in love with," I exaggerated the word 'love,' "and I happen to know the kid, too. He's a fuckin', excuse me, retard; wound up in the alternative school and has a part-time job rimming tires. She didn't even give me a chance to ask her out. So, I had to settle on, you know, second best."

"Second best?"

"Yeah. This one wasn't as hot. But, I found out that she was experienced. I think more experienced with sex than I was." I regret saying the last part, but it's too late.

"How old were you, at the time?"

"We were both eighteen." I add that it was last summer, so Georgia'll think that I'm much more experienced, now.

"Did you have sex with her, then?"

"Yeah," I say casually, "we went to a movie. Instead of me taking my old pickup, my dad let me drive his Buick. I usually borrowed it for important dates. After the movie, we both decided to park for a while and make-out. Then it just, like, happened."

"What happened?" She puts her legal pad to one side and tilts her head.

I try to look away from her, but I can't. Our eyes are locked together and I'm not, for some reason, embarrassed anymore. But, still, my words stumble out.

"We had sex. We changed places. I sat in the passenger seat and she sat in my lap, facing me, her knees clamped my hips. She chewed her gum faster and as we frenched, I tried to find her gum, but she, like, had it hidden somewhere. I searched just about every tooth, with my tongue and still couldn't find it. We were having

54

fun doing this, when she leaned against me, smiled and whispered, 'Do you wanna do it?' I always carry a condom in my wallet, so I said, 'sure!'"

"I hate to stop you there, really I do, but our time's up," Georgia says, her disappointment seems sincere. "We'll pick up where we left off, okay?"

She puts her hand on my shoulder, as we walk out the door. She's about the same height as I am, maybe an inch shorter. The perfume she's wearing has the light, pleasant fragrance of cherry blossoms. Georgia moves her hand from my shoulder to the back of my neck. It feels warm.

"See you next week," she says. I nod. She looks tired.

On my way out, I read the building's directory that's on the wall by the front door and find: "Georgia A. Moore, LICSW, Mental Health Therapist … Rm 107."

I study the word, Therapist. I say it slowly, then divide it into two words, THE … RAPIST. I whisper the words and catch myself smiling. Even though I can feel Mel's stare boring into me, I don't turn to look at him. He's probably wondering why I'm seeing Georgia. Maybe the old fart's jealous. I hope so.

I actually look forward to our fifth session. It's drizzling rain, for now, but there's a promise of a thunderstorm, later. Before I go in, I take a long drag off my cigarette and flip it away. It hisses when it hits the sidewalk. Shit, I realize that I could've finished the rest of the cigarette under the building canopy, then put it in the butt can, conveniently standing next to the door. Oh, well.

I knock once on her door. She surprises me by opening it immediately.

"Hi, Jason, come on in."

I want to call her Georgia, to test her, but decide against it. Just like teachers, there's a barrier you can't cross.

"Hi, Miss Moore." She's wearing a tan skirt, a couple of inches above the knee, with a pastel, orange top. We sit.

"Tell me more about that girl. Did she have a name?"

"No. I mean, I forgot."

"That's okay," she says, as she looks over at the three, gray filing cabinets, against the wall. I imagine that they're full of yellow notepads. "Go ahead."

"The girl's, like, rubbing up against me," I begin, "and I start to unbutton her shirt. When I get done with that, she asks me if I want to unhook her bra. I reach up her back, but can't find the hook and she laughs and says that this one unhooks in the front. Then, she unhooks it herself and her tit ... I mean, boobs, kind of, spring out toward my face. Really nice boobs, not huge, but perfectly shaped. I cupped them in my hands and, like, ran my thumbs over her hard nipples. She unbuttons my shirt and we start rubbing against each other. Warm skin on warm skin. A distant street light shines across our writhing bodies. She slips off of me into the driver's seat and slides her jeans off along with her panties. I start to follow her lead and unzip my jeans, too.

"'No, let me do that,'" she says, like she's out of breath. She gets on the floor in front of me and pulls my pants down to my ankles. My jockey shorts were next. She's smiling, the gum-chewing speeds up, as she slowly slides my underwear down. The end of my cock gets hung-up on the elastic waistband, she giggles and takes her time freeing it. When she finally frees it, I feel it slap against my belly.

"She gets on top again. I roll the condom on and she positions my throbbing prick under her and, like, eases down on it. I start pumping like a maniac, but she whispers, 'slow down. Let me do the work.' I'm thinking that she's done this lots of times before. She rides me, first slowly, then fast, then slow again and leans into me and, like, groans into my ear. I feel her hot breath, when, suddenly, my body starts jerking and I feel like I'm gonna pass out. Her eyes widen and all she says is, 'oh!' like she's either surprised or disappointed."

I stop talking when I realize too late, that the girl didn't say, "oh!" the voice belongs to Georgia.

I lean forward, my legs are crossed and blurt out, "Why'd you make me tell you that?"

"I didn't make you do anything."

"It don't have anything to do with lycanthropy!" I protest.

She smiles, "That's very interesting," and glances at a bookshelf across the room. It's filled with all kinds of textbooks that have to do with her job; all the answers to all the questions in the Universe.

"Do you know what lycanthropy actually means?"

"Sure I do. It's when somebody turns into a werewolf."

"Well, not exactly. It's a delusional system, or mental illness, in which someone thinks they turn into a werewolf."

I can't believe it, but I start to cry and I never cry in front of other people and I shouldn't, especially in front of Georgia. I lean forward, my hands are pressed against my face and it feels hot. I look up at her, tears stream down my cheeks.

She nods. "It's all right, Jason." She comes over and sits beside me on the couch, rubs and pats my back and repeats that it's all right. She tries to help me up, but I'm not ready to stand because my goddam shlong gets stiff, again. She runs her fingers through my hair, which doesn't help.

"You can stand up when you're ready," she says, knowingly, "our session is over, anyway."

Ignoring the box of tissues she hands me, I wipe my tears with my fingers. I stand up like I'm eighty years old, tired and shaky. There's a wet spot, the size of a quarter, on the front of my pants. I lean toward her, my right hip presses against her left. This is the closest I ever got to Georgia. It feels good and I smell cherry blossoms.

She steps away and says, "Werewolf, huh? I've got an idea. Instead of coming here on Monday, I think we can schedule a session on Thursday night. There's supposed to be a full moon that night and it'll test that theory of yours."

"I don't know," I mumble, "I mean, are you sure you want to do this? It'll be, like, dangerous."

"Don't worry," she smiles sweetly, "you can come after work, let's say at nine-thirty."

"Okay, but I won't be looking forward to it and neither should you."

It's Thursday night and I arrive a little early. The sun set a few minutes ago and the moon is beginning to rise. The temperature's going down a little, but the humidity still makes it hard to breathe.

I start walking down the hall, when Mel stops me.

"You can't do in there now, she's got a client," he rasps.

That's it! I turn back and walk toward his desk. He leans back in his chair and glares at me. I glare back, pacing in front of him. He crosses his arms over his chest like a big, fat, fuckin' Sultan.

All my muscles grow and tighten and I feel sudden strength coursing through my body. I'm burning with adrenalin. Then, I lunge across Mel's desk, bearing my teeth. I want to rip his head off and scatter pieces of him all over the lobby.

Mel lifts his bulk out of the chair and shouts, "Stupid kid!" And with an overhand right, hits me with a large, meaty fist across the bridge of my nose. It knocks me to the floor. I put my hand to my nose and prop myself up on one elbow.

"Shit!" I yell, as Mel comes out from behind the desk.

Georgia must've heard the commotion because I hear somebody running, then see her kneeling down beside me. She slips her arm under my head. Blood is gushing from my nose, getting all over me and all over her skirt. She doesn't seem to care about bloodstains. Then to someone I can't see, she shouts, "Soak some paper towels in cold water and bring them here!" She yells at someone else to call the police. My eyes are swelling up and I can barely see, but I notice a short Latina trying to get behind Mel's desk to use the phone.

"Get the hell out of the way!" Georgia screams at Mel, then adds, "Mel, you stupid fuck, I think you broke his nose!" Mel's lips move, but nothing comes out.

Finally, his voice shaking, "He came at me. It was self-defense."

Georgia responds with an offering, "Get fucked! He's a client of mine, you asshole!"

Mel jams his hands into his pockets.

"Policia are coming," the Latina tells Georgia, who nods.

Georgia leans over me. Her glasses almost fall off the top of her head, but she catches them. Tears well-up in her eyes and I watch a drop fall toward my face. She flashes a glance at Mel and says between clenched teeth, "Listen, Mel, this is the last job you'll ever have, understand? Stupid bastard!"

Two burly cops fling the front door open and ask, urgently, "What's going on here?"

"That clown," Georgia points her thumb at Mel, "assaulted my client and broke his nose."

Both cops rush Mel, spin him around and snap handcuffs on him. "Do you want me to send an ambulance?" one of the cops ask.

Georgia waves her hand, "No, I'm taking him to the hospital, myself."

"Are you sure?"

"Yes, I'm sure."

"Is anybody gonna press charges?"

"Yes, I'll have my lawyer contact you," Georgia answers.

The cops roll their eyes and push Mel out the door while quoting his Miranda rights.

"Jason, can you stand up? Maria, can you help me get him up?"

"Sure, sure, of course." Maria, the short Latina rushes over. Evidently, she's either one of Georgia's clients, or one of the cleaners.

"Hold the towels to your face, Jason, and don't hold your head back."

With an arm around my waist, she guides me to her car. My whole face is on fire with pain and yet it feels numb. I worry about how my nose looks and imagine it twice its normal size and smashed flat.

"Are we going to the hospital?" my words come out muffled.

"No, I'm taking you to my house. I'll see what I can do for you there. At the hospital, you might have to sit in the waiting room for a couple of hours before anyone gets around to seeing you. Don't worry. It'll be okay. I feel that I'm responsible for what happened to you and I'm so sorry. There's just no excuse for Mel's behavior. He's a retired cop who missed bullying people, so he became a security guard. That son of a bitch is absolutely soulless. We can probably sue his company out of existence."

Her words seem comforting in a way, but I'm confused about what happened. There's a full moon, but I'm the one who got hurt.

The stoplight changes fast; amber to red and she brakes hard. I'm thrown forward. Goddam it," I yell. My nose throbs even more.

"Oh, shit, I'm sorry," she looks at me with a pained look of sincere, not practiced, concern.

"I'm kinda disappointed that I didn't turn into a werewolf."

"I am, too ... kind of," she allows herself a tiny laugh, then adds seriously, "How're you doing?"

"Okay, just don't make any more sudden stops."

"Hang on, we're almost there."

We drive up to the doors of an underground parking garage beneath a large, condo complex. She swipes an access card and the massive doors open. After she swipes her card again, we enter a vestibule leading to a pair of elevators.

"I'm on the fourth floor," Georgia speaks, but I'm not really paying much attention. I'm dizzy and have to lean on the elevator wall.

"This way," she points down the hallway. "After I get you settled in, I'll have to make some phone calls."

Using her card, I hear a metallic click and she opens the door. I'm ushered into a large, master bedroom.

"Lie down here. I'll get another pillow."

"But, the blood ..."

"It's dried, now. Here, give me those paper towels and I'll put some ice into a real towel."

She disappears into the master bath and returns with a wet cloth and gently wipes my face. I automatically wince when she does this, even though I don't feel anything. Then she applies the icepack.

"I'm sorry," she tells me, "but you're going to have two black eyes. If you want to watch TV, the remote's on the night stand."

A small TV sits on the corner of a dresser and I think about turning it on, but change my mind. What if her husband, if she's really married, or her boyfriend, if she's not, comes home and finds me here. He'll probably be pissed! He'll kick my ass and throw me outta here. Then, Georgia'll yell at him, "What the hell do you think you're doing, Mike?" His name's probably Mike ... or Joey. Then,

60

he'll say that he owns half the house and she'll tell him to fuck off. She can say this because she makes more in one hour than he makes in eight. He threatens to punch her and she runs and gets an iron frying pan and creases his skull with it and kills him. Me and Georgia have to run away to South America.

I snap out of the half-dream when Georgia comes back into the room.

"Here, try to sit up and take this Ibuprofen. By the way, I called your mother; told her that you'd fallen down the steps at my office building and said for her not to worry. She's going to call your work, tomorrow."

"And she bought that?"

"She seemed to, but your dad was upset and said that the building was unsafe."

Apparently, Georgia didn't tell them that her office is on the first floor.

"I also called my lawyer," she adds without elaborating further.

"Were you ever, like, married?"

She looks away, "Why do you ask?"

"Just curious."

"Yes, I was. We were divorced about a year ago; married a short time, no kids."

"So, did he live here?"

"Yes."

"Is he ever coming back, like, for a surprise visit?"

"No, he moved far away. Do you think that you'd be more comfortable if you got undressed and slipped under the covers?"

I hesitate, "I don't know …"

"It's all right. I'm going to be sleeping on the couch in the living room."

"Well, okay then."

"It's a good thing I canceled my appointments for tomorrow because you and I are going shopping to buy you some new clothes. The clothes you have on are ruined and I'm going to throw them away."

"If you throw my clothes away, how can I go shopping with you?"

"Good point! I'll just have to shop without you. Now, take those clothes off and leave them on the floor. I'll get them in the morning. Try to get some rest."

"Wait a minute, Miss Moore. I'm gonna need some help getting this t-shirt off." I hope that she'll correct on the "Miss Moore" part.

"First of all, in private you may call me, Georgia."

Yes, yes yes! I finally cracked the barrier! "Georgia," I say over and over in my head. "How'd you wind up with a name like Georgia?"

"It's because my dad wanted a boy named after him. His name's George."

"That makes sense. So, was your husband's last name, Moore?"

"No, I went back to my maiden name. Sit up and put your arms over your head. Wait, I've got a better idea. I'll cut your shirt off with a scissors."

I look at the rust colored, crusty, stained mess. It's all over the front of me. The ice in the towel is melting, so I take it off.

She comes back into the room, "No, you have to keep the ice on your face."

"But, it's melting. What're you trying to do, waterboard me? Just kidding."

She returns with a dry towel full of ice. She's changed into a fluffy, white bathrobe.

"Keep this on your face. It'll keep the swelling down."

The scissors cut down the front of my shirt and I slip my arms out. She sits down on the bed and her ass touches my hip. My damn dick comes to life.

"Now, for your pants," she says, nonchalantly.

"Georgia …" My voice trails off. I decide to let her do whatever she wants.

She starts to unbutton my 501s, slowly, one by one and accidentally on purpose, touches my rod with her arm. At least I think it's her arm. I arch up, so she can get them past my ass. Then,

I lift my legs up, she takes hold of the cuffs and pulls them off. I lift a corner of the icepack and peek out. She's looking at my jockeys and tells me that she'll have to buy underwear for me, too.

If she's looking at my underwear, she'd have to be blind not to notice my cock at attention.

"Keep that icepack on," she reminds me.

She leans across me and runs her finger through my hair, like she did before and this time, she adds a kiss on my forehead. Her lips are warm. Her tongue is on my lips and I open my mouth, willingly and force my tongue deep into her mouth. I feel her body moving up.

"Georgia?"

She moves her fingertip back and forth, across my lips, so I shut up. I peek again, from under the icepack and discover that it's not her fingertip, it's one of her nipples.

"Holy shit," I catch myself saying it aloud and open my mouth to take her in. She alternates breasts until her nipples are rock-hard. Her breathing gets rapid. She reaches down, pulls off my underwear and tosses them on the floor, "Georgia," I moan.

She massages my balls and gives a couple of jerks on my joint before taking me into her mouth. Her tongue and mouth are soft, warm and wet. She begins slow and then, goes faster. My entire body is, like, full of electricity and starts to shake. She knows exactly when to stop and finishes me off with her hand. I slide my hand up under her robe, up her thigh and my finger probes inside of her. I find out that she's just as soft, warm and wet there, too.

She takes my hand away and coos, "Tomorrow, definitely tomorrow."

I wake up the next morning, naked and lying next to a soggy towel. I hear Georgia's voice coming from the kitchen, at the far end of the condo. She's on the phone, standing naked. She looks me up and down because I'm naked, too and puts a finger up to her lips. I lean against a counter and listen.

She's talking to Mom. "Yes, Mrs. Conroy, I think that Jason is progressing nicely and if we increase our sessions to twice a week, it may be more beneficial. Yes, twice a week would be the treatment plan I'd recommend. No, I don't think drug therapy is the answer because his case, I believe, isn't that severe. I know, Mrs. Conroy, but we are making progress. He's beginning to react more positively now. When he comes home, you'll see the change in him, I'm sure of it.

Mondays and we'll add Thursdays. On the matter of his accident, he's recovering nicely. I'm thinking of sending him home, tomorrow. All right, Mrs. Conroy, goodbye."

"Jason, I almost lost it when you came in here," she laughs.

Neither one of us tries to cover up our parts and I'm standing here with another stiffy, as I study a real woman's body. I don't know if she customizes her pubes, but it's a perfect triangle of light, brown hair, much like the hair on her head, without the blond highlights.

"You're gonna have me come in for sessions twice a week?"

"Jason, what difference does it make? Your parents make the co-pay, anyway."

"Oh yeah, that's right." We both laugh, hysterically.

"C'mon, big boy." She takes me by the hand. "How do you feel?"

"Horny, but can I look in the mirror, first?"

"No, not yet. We've got some business to take care of."

Back to the bedroom. I find a condom in my wallet and slip it on. She's on her back and I slide inside of her. I begin at arm's length and wind up on my elbows pumping hard. Our bellies slap together. She thrusts her hips in unison with mine. I feel my body tremble. It's over and I roll off of her, breathing hard. I start laughing because it's so good. I ask her if she thinks it was good and she says that I "need more training," but that it was still "okay." Then, I watch intently as she brings herself to orgasm. Her muscles tense, she arches her back, holds her breath and then, collapses like a carnival tent, when the show's over.

She props herself up on an elbow, "I need to go shopping. Stay here and rest."

Maybe Mel beat me to death and I'm in heaven.

After she leaves, I go into the bathroom to check on my nose in the mirror. Oh, fuck! It looks like a mangled bratwurst. It also looks soft, but when I touch it, it's hard. It's throbbing like it has its own pulse, but the throbbing isn't as bad as it was before. And I have two, swollen, black eyes. I wish, now, that Mel had given me an uppercut to the stomach.

I turn on the TV, find the Court Channel and with the soft droning of their voices, I fall asleep.

Georgia touches me and I wake up.

"Hi. I got you some clothes, exactly like the ones you had and a pair of sunglasses. I hope the glasses fit you." She studies the width of my nose.

"Thanks, babe," I try out that word and look for a reaction. She seems pleased with it.

"I also got you a bottle of saline to squirt up your nose, so you can get rid of the dried blood and you can breathe better."

I'm thinking that I want to smell cherry blossoms.

"There's something we need to talk about," suddenly, she's all serious. "Do you know that if you tell anyone about what we're doing, I could lose my license?

"What license?"

"My license to practice. My therapist's license. The 'L' in LICSW stands for licensed."

"I won't, Georgia, I promise. How could I ever do that to you?"

"People do. It's like blackmail, Jason. If something goes wrong with the relationship ... "

"What could go wrong with us?"

"Nothing, I guess."

"You wanna do it again?"

She laughs and says, "Sure, why not? Oh, I forgot to mention that I bought twenty-five condoms. For you, it's only a week's supply. I don't know what it is, but I just can't get enough of you." She stops and thinks for a second, then says, "Actually, I *do* know what it is."

She slowly, teasingly strips in front of me, then gets on top. I hear her inhale through her teeth, like an asthmatic snake.

She rolls off when we're done and staring at the ceiling says, "I think, sexually, we're a pretty close match. I'm at my sexual peak and so are you. You're able to get an erection about every ten minutes. Most men my age, are lucky if they can get it up, once."

"I'm just a kid and you're probably ten years older … "

"Twelve," she responds.

"Okay, twelve. So, why do you want to mess around with a kid? Don't, like, get me wrong or anything … "

"You're not a kid, you're an attractive man. We need to get you dressed and I'll take you to the doctor." Before I get a chance to ask why, she explains, "My lawyer said that we need a medical report in case it goes to court, although, he didn't think it would, because these companies usually settle out of court. You know, to avoid adverse publicity. Why don't you try that saline, first? Then I'll help you get your t-shirt on."

The first thing the doctor says is, "Who did this to you?" Then, he orders an x-ray. It's broken, all right, but the doc says that it might turn out normal-looking, just a little wider across the bridge of the nose. But, if I wanted him to, he could recommend a plastic surgeon. "It's just something to think about," he adds. I tell him that the saline helps and he only nods. "Now, I'm going to put a piece of white tape across your nose. It doesn't help anything. It's just to remind you to take it easy."

Georgia asks me if I want to go home today. I tell her no, maybe tomorrow. She drives us to a restaurant to have lunch. I put on the aviator-style sunglasses she gave me. They seem heavy on my tender nose.

It's one of those family-type restaurants where they serve breakfast and lunch all day and close at supper time. To me, that never made any sense. Every bright light in the place is on, so I'm glad I'm wearing sunglasses. There's a sign saying to seat ourselves and we head to a booth.

A young waitress appears and slides laminated menus in front of us. She interrupts herself announcing the specials of the day and stares at my nose. "My god! What happened to your face?" She looks first at me, then at Georgia for an answer, who's studying the menu and not paying attention. Even though I could tell her that it's none of her business, I answer anyway.

"I was playing baseball. A grounder came at me and it, like, took a bad hop."

66

"And it hit you in the face," she finishes the answer for me, "that's too bad. Do you wanna start off with coffee?"

Georgia look up, "Yes, two black coffees."

I order a burger with fries and Georgia orders scrambled eggs with toast and hash browns.

The food comes and I take a bite out of my burger. I let it drop to the plate because I can't taste or smell. I don't care about taste, I just wanna be able to smell and I want to smell her.

The waitress rushes back, "Sir, is there anything wrong with your order?" her eyes dart back and forth between Georgia and me.

"No," we answer in unison.

"I can't taste or smell anything," I explain to Georgia.

"Well, you have to eat something, you're too skinny as it is."

I dismiss what she says and tell her that I'm in great shape then, change the subject. "Why do you still have me coming to you for therapy?"

"Because we have a lot more work to do."

"Like more training?" I ask, grinning.

"Yes, something like that," she answers with a wry smile and a wink.

"I think you cured me of, like, being a werewolf."

She turns serious, "I don't cure people. Although, you might be feeling a little better about yourself, now. Do you?"

"Yeah, I guess."

"And I think you'll be able to control the werewolf behavior much easier, now. On the way home, I'm going to stop at the drugstore for a few things."

She already bought some condoms, so I hate to ask her what else she needed, but did anyway. "What else do you need?"

"It's not for me, it's for you. A razor and some shaving crème." She slides her finger down the side of my face. "You're a blond, so I can hardly see your whiskers, but they're all prickly," she says, shooting me an expression that I've never seen before— squinched-up eyes and wrinkled nose. I run my own fingers across the stubble on my chin.

"And some deodorant."

The last one floors me. Does she think I stink? Maybe, 'cause I can't smell myself. She leans forward and takes my hand like she's gonna tell me a deep, dark secret. It's two-thirty in the afternoon and there's only five other people in the place.

"When we get back to my house, you can shave and shower. Would you like it if I joined you in the shower?"

"Wow, of course I would!" I can wait a little while, but my cock is already on duty.

"Just remember, Jason, you do not tell anyone about what we're doing. It might get back to your mother." Just the mention of Mom makes my dick shrivel, like a turtle instinctively pulling its head back into its shell whenever it senses danger.

"That's not gonna happen, Georgia."

"No matter what?"

"No matter what."

As we walk to her car, I reach into my jeans pocket for my pack of cigarettes and pull one out. I have to finish it outside while she runs the air conditioner. About twenty minutes later, we were in the shower, soaping each other up.

We have sex afterwards and she says it's better this time. I'm happy that I'm getting trained by the best teacher I ever had. I flash back to my seventh grade English teacher. Take that, Mrs. Trench!

Georgia brings out a shoebox full of DVDs and asks me if I like comedy or drama. I ask if she has *Meet the Fockers*. She does and we settle in bed to watch it. She's in her white bathrobe and I'm in my underwear. After the movie, she opens her robe and invites me in.

Suddenly, it seems, it's Saturday and I beg to stay another day. She says, "No," because she already told Mom that I'd be home today. Georgia drives me to her office parking lot and parks next to my pickup. After a long French kiss, she whispers, "See you Monday," and I reluctantly watch her drive off.

I'm glad that when I get home, there's nobody here. I turn on the TV and wait for them. A few minutes later, they noisily enter the house. Jordan comes running into the living room first and it looks as if she's going to run past, but comes to a screeching halt in front of me.

"What happened to you?"

Mom appears at Jordan's side. "Take off those sunglasses," she says, "let me see." She lets out a gasp. "I'll get some ice." I tell her no, that it'll be okay. Then, Dad comes hobbling in.

His angry mood contrasts with his pathetic appearance as he stands, leaning with both hands on his cane. He's only in his early forties, but he looks, ten, maybe twenty years older. It seems that he's getting balder every day. His shirt hangs out of his pants to minimize the fact that his stomach hangs over his belt.

They stand in front of me like Larry, Moe and Curly. In my imagination, Mom is always Moe. I catch myself as I almost say, Georgia. "Miss Moore took me to the doctor. It's broken."

"For the chrissakes," Dad says to both me and Mom, "why don't that building have an elevator?"

"It's not the building's fault, Dave," Mom says.

"Yeah, Dave," Jordan sings, mockingly, then runs away to avoid Dad's attempt to cuff her.

"Have you had anything to eat?" Mom asks.

"Yeah," I lie, "I stopped at Mac and Don's." I'm not the least bit hungry and can wait 'til dinnertime. Without another word, Mom stalks into the kitchen. Dad motions for me to come outside with him. We stand on the front steps and light cigarettes.

He stares at the clouds, takes a long drag, blows it out fast and says, "I can't believe you're that clumsy ... falling down the steps." I laugh and remind him that he wasn't there to see it. "Well," he adds, "is that woman, your therapist, doin' you any good?"

I look away. I don't want him to see me smirking. I feel like saying that she's doin' me real good, instead say, "Yeah, I think so."

"And I think that she's goin' an extra mile with you ... taking you to her house and the doctor and convincin' me and your mother that you need two sessions a week."

I feel a little bit guilty, because it's costing them more, but the feeling passes. "That's what her plan is," I tell him, as he lets out a heavy sigh of resignation.

"Whaddya tell her about us?" he asks, concerned.

"I can't tell ya, it's confidential."

"Confidential!" he snorts, with a tone dripping with condescension. He shuffles and turns awkwardly toward the door. I open it for him. That's all he does is walk away from everything … from life itself. I sit on the steps and smoke another cigarette. I can't wait 'til Monday when Georgia and me get to fuck each other's brains out.

Mercifully, Monday afternoon comes fast. I smoke a last cigarette under the shade of the building's canopy. I see a new security guard, a young, black guy, about my age, sitting at Mel's desk. I check in with him and even though I know where I'm going, he stands and points down the hallway. I nod politely. This time, Georgia greets me outside of her door wearing a serious expression. I wish that's all she's wearing. She gives me an obligatory smile … a smile, I imagine she gives to all her clients. I'm a little confused by this.

I sit on the couch and gaze at her. "Did you ever make it in your chair?"

"This is a regular therapy session. Could you be an adult?" She looks down at her notes. "Let's see, you hate your mother and your sister. You think they're bossy bitches and you barely tolerate your father because you think he's weak, but on some level, you feel sorry for him. And your lycanthropy," she stares intently at me when she says that word, "is a defense mechanism you employ for protection."

"Who am I supposed to be protecting?"

"Yourself, against everything you believe is evil, like people who are mean to you. And you know what happens when you approach women your age for sex?" she asks rhetorically, "you want them to make the first move and when they don't, you force yourself to make it, risking rejection. When you get older, I think that you'll handle rejection, easier. Have I got just about everything right?"

I just sit in silence, my jaw drops open and with my eyes bulging. I do the nearly impossible, I swallow hard, with my mouth open. I tell myself that she's fuckin' brilliant. "Is that why, with me, you, like, made the first move?"

"No, but that doesn't make me a slut or a sexual predator, does it?"

70

"No!" I almost yell, defensively, "I, like, never thought that at all! You're a good person!"

"Will you do me a favor, Jason? Do you think you can stop saying 'like' all the time? You really don't need to say it."

"Like, okay, Mrs. Trench."

"Inside joke?" she asks and I fill her in on the joke. "While we're on the topic of sex, you had asked if I ever 'made it in my chair.' The answer is no." When she uncrosses her legs, she hikes up her skirt so I can see she's not wearing any underwear. I practically run over to her, almost tripping over the coffee table.

She stands and spins me into her chair and yanks my pants off. The chair's big enough, so she's able to straddle me. I take an ever-present condom out of my wallet. After we finish, she goes over and sits on the couch. Now, I feel like I'm the therapist.

"Have you ever made it on the coffee table?" I ask. She tells me that it wouldn't hold both of us.

Suddenly, she looks at the clock and says, "Shit, I've got another client in three minutes! You have to leave!"

I stand and pull my pants up and she reaches under the chair cushion and pulls out her panties. I watch her put them on.

"I mean it, you have to leave. I'll see you on Thursday."

As usual, I tell her that I can't wait. Another client is scheduled after me. She had told me that sometimes it happens in case we have a date and she's late.

Thursday rolls around and I find myself being able to breathe a little better. It also means that I can finally taste and smell. The crescent shapes, under my eyes are beginning to change from black to a yellowish green.

I'm surprised to see Georgia standing at the front desk, talking to the guard. "I had a cancellation," she explains. I'm jealous at first, but then realize that she talks to other people all day long. She rushes down the hall ahead of me.

As soon as I walk into her office, she closes the door behind me and locks it. "Are you ready for your session?"

I answer playfully, "Oh, yeah! Are you ready for yours?"

She laughs loudly, "We've got plenty of time. You're my last client today. By the way, I have to see someone on Saturday."

"You have to work on Saturday?"

"No, you jerk, I just have to see you! Preferably at my place. If you can't remember my address, I'll write it down. Now let's get started, shall we?"

"Didja ever make it on your couch?"

She shakes her head and flings herself onto it and I dive on top of her. After that, she clears the top of her desk and we do it on its surface, with her sitting on top of me. She tells me, as if I don't know that's a good idea to put on a new condom each time.

Afterwards, we stay naked and talk for a while. She lets me smoke in her office and that's the only concession she makes. I'm not allowed to smoke in her house. As we get dressed, she reminds me that we have a date on Saturday.

I call her on Saturday morning and ask if I can come over right away. She says that afternoon is better, but when I sound disappointed, she says to come over at about ten-thirty.

She picks out an ancient movie for us to watch. It's called, *Inherit the Wind*. It's all about religion and evolution. I don't recognize any of the actors, but the two main characters are pretty good.

We have sex three times before she tells me that I should go home because she doesn't want Mom to worry about me. There goes a possible fourth time, as soon as she mentions Mom. Talk about coitus interruptus!

On the following Monday, she informs me that she started her period yesterday. So, we just talk. On Thursday, we talk and then she offers to give me a blowjob. I accept, of course. It's better than my job at the supermarket.

The next week, my nose feels better and she says it's okay for me to give her some oral and after that, I ask her if she's ever done it on her Persian rug. She replies that she hadn't and that it's a fake Persian. We move the coffee table aside and she gets on top of me. At first, she leans back and fingers herself, while she moves up and down with long, even strokes, then lies down as close as she can and pumps while we French each other. When we're done, she rolls off. We're both panting and sweating. I touch the sweat on my chest, our sweat, mingled together, hers a cherry blossom scent and mine, just plain, old sweat.

She lies on her back, looking at the ceiling. "We've done it in every place in this room, you know that?" she asks, wistfully.

"Does oral count, Georgia?"

"Yes."

"Then we even did it on the wall. The only place we haven't done it is on the ceiling."

She looks at me and says, "We can't."

"Gravity?"

"Yes, otherwise I suppose we'd try it." She rolls onto her side to face me. "You're the best," she tells me and touches my face.

It's a real boost to my self-respect, not to mention, my self-confidence. But, the long-time lack of both, makes me ask, "Are you sure? Do you really mean that?"

She rolls over on top of me and purrs, "Of course I do."

She asks me if my parents know that I'm dating someone and I inform her that they suspect it. She tells me to tell them that I am and she's somebody they don't know. And if they press further, she advises to tell them that everything's all right and not to be concerned.

At the next opportunity, I tell my folks. As expected, Mom pushes for more information. Dad steps in, "Will you cool it, Midge? Let the boy have a life!" I'm shocked that Dad stands up to her, for once.

It turns out that therapy sessions twice a week aren't enough for either Georgia or me. Sometimes, she invites me over to her place, or sometimes we go to a restaurant, or out to a movie. She's says that we're becoming co-dependent, but she also says that it's not entirely a bad thing.

In the past few months, we both avoid using the "L" word, even though it's on our minds and we come very close to saying it several times. I ask myself if that means that we're both afraid of commitment. I ask Georgia about it and she says that we have a wonderful sex life, why ruin it by saying we love each other. Then, I come right out anyway and tell her that I love her.

She grabs and hugs me hard. "Jason, I must be crazy for saying this, but I love you, too." I easily imagine myself married to her, but I don't let her know that.

We make love a couple of times in her bed, when she asks me what I'm going to do with my life. I answer like I know exactly what she means. "I'm going to get an A.A. degree, then go on to a four-year college."

"What about your job at the supermarket?"

"Are you jokin'? I wanna dump that job, just as soon as I graduate in a year and a half and it'll be sooner than that, if I keep going during the summer."

"Okay, you'll eventually have a four-year degree, then what?"

I can't figure out why she's grilling me like this and I finally say, "After that, I'll marry you."

I immediately regret saying it and turn my face to the wall.

She comes up behind me and drapes an arm across my chest, "Jason, I'm flattered that you said that, so don't feel embarrassed."

"It seems that I'm always saying the wrong things."

"I don't think so. Your mother said that your therapy can't last much longer. I think that it's a matter of money. So, our sessions will have to end soon."

"What'll we do then?"

"Oh, I didn't mean to imply that we can't see each other anymore. And about marrying me; I can't marry a client, it's against the rules."

"So, what I hear you saying, is that you're not allowed to marry me if I remain a client?"

She raises an eyebrow and tells me that I should become a therapist. "This is what I'm saying," she emphatically adds. "Besides, I don't want to get married to anyone, right now. This career of mine already cost me one husband."

I try to control my voice, but it trembles and tears start rolling down my cheeks. "But, why don't you wanna marry me?"

"Didn't I already tell you? I can't. Please don't get the impression that I've led you on. I really do enjoy being with you and we can continue being with each other as boyfriend and girlfriend."

74

"Oh sure," I snap back.

"Look, Jason, I think that eventually you'll want to meet someone like me, who's your own age and marry *her*."

Why is she saying this to me, especially after we just made love? "Georgia, are you saying that I'm not mature enough for you? Was your ex-husband mature? Why did he divorce you?"

"And why do you assume that he divorced me? I divorced him. Do you want to know why?"

I sigh and say, "Go ahead and tell me."

"We both took our careers, our professions seriously, only he thought that his was more important."

"What did he do?" I interrupt.

"He was an investment banker. He's probably looking for another job, right now. There were other reasons why we couldn't stand each other, as well."

I blink back tears and my nose is running, so I wipe it with the back of my hand. "I think I understand that if we got married, my mom would somehow find out and make a huge federal case out of the fact that I, like, married my therapist. You'd lose your license, for sure. My mom is just evil!"

"I think that she only wants to protect you. Not that you need protection from me. Perhaps, you actually need protection from her."

Even though she's sincere when she says this, I turn to her and laugh. She always knows how to cheer me up. She explains that we'll go on seeing each other for as long as I want. Then, she surprises me by saying that she wants me to move in with her. I mean, what the fuck? The way she was going, I thought she wanted to dump me. I'll be thrilled just to get away from my dysfunctional family and I'll be looking forward to being with Georgia every day.

I take her face in my hands and gently kiss her.

"See?" she assures me, everything turned out okay."

"So, do ya wanna do it, I mean, make love again?" she nods.

After that, she rolls over and dozes off. I get up and tiptoe to her living room to where her bookcase is and find a dictionary. I came to the realization, a long time ago, that she's a nympho; addicted to sex. Hopefully, addicted to sex with me. I start wondering if I'm a sex addict, too. I look up "Sat ... Saty ... *Satyriasis*."

I read it, smile to myself, then snap the book shut.

ontrariety

y name is Mrs. Denise Mortensen and I'm a psychiatric nurse at County General, seventh floor. One of my favorite patients had been diagnosed with dissociative identity disorder. Today, when I talked with Mike, he decided to become a philosophy professor and believes that I'm his secretary.

Mike speaks in an affected British accent, one that he liked when he called himself, "King of the London Stage." Since he thinks that we're both English, I speak to him with the same accent, which I don't mind. I find it actually charming. I also like it that he calls me "Salts."

Presently, I remind him that he has an appointment with the staff psychiatrist, whom he thinks is a physics professor.

"Salts, shall I wear my camel hair tweed, today?"

"I think not, Sir, it's rather warm."

"Fine. I'll wear my linen jacket. Necktie or ascot?"

"Necktie."

"Well, I'm off, then."

I want to say, "You certainly are," but hold my tongue. I don't want to make him angry, although I'm sure he's harmless.

"How did your meeting go, Professor?"

"All right, I imagine. You know old Knox, daft as usual. And drinking before noon! I know it's Saturday, but my god! I hope I never get that way. Poor, old sod."

"I can positively assure you that you will never get that way."

"Thank you, Salts. Whatever shall I do without you? Do I have any afternoon appointments?"

"You have a three o'clock with Dr. Peterson and after that, *I* get to have you all to myself for an entire hour."

"Correction. Only fifty minutes, Salts."

"And Monday morning, Professor, don't forget about your meeting with that ex-Rugby player. What's his name?"

"Miles."

"That's right. You were teammates with him on the Manchester Lions in the 1950s. He told me that you played hard, as if you were possessed."

"That would be a neat trick since I was born in the seventies. And, by the way, I've never played Rugby."

"Oh, sorry. I must have been thinking of someone else. Perhaps and old beau. Well, what sport did you play?"

"I played tennis when I attended university. Was incredibly bad at it. Why do you ask?"

"I don't know. It just popped into my head."

My name is Dr. Michael Bradford and I am a staff psychiatrist at County General in Boston. I was educated at Cambridge University in London. Mrs. Denise Mortensen has been in my care and has been since I arrived four years ago. At that time, I diagnosed her condition as dissociative identity disorder. She believes that I'm someone else with the same condition as hers and this week she believes that she works at this hospital as a psychiatric nurse and that I am a patient here. Mrs. Mortensen does not realize that my office is not a hospital room. Furthermore, she is severely delusional in that she invents identities for me, as well.

Her adult children had her committed to this hospital which she insists is in London. In addition, she always speaks in an English accent. I have tried to talk to her in a faux American accent in an attempt to bring some portion of her life back to reality, to no avail.

Her real identity is so repressed that even under hypnosis, I cannot bring it out. She is completely harmless, so I do not have any concerns in that regard and have allowed her access to the common areas of the ward.

"Mike, can we talk now?"

"Oh, Salts, you startled me. Do you mind my asking where you got the scissors and what do you plan to do with them?"

"Give you a haircut. What else would I do?"

"I recently had a … oh, maybe a little trim, then. Where did you learn to cut hair?"

"I had brothers. I had to use a different size bowl for each of their heads."

"Well, Salts … perhaps another time. Why don't you put the scissors down on my desk."

"That's not a desk! It's a nightstand!"

A s the on duty psychiatric nurse, I was making my usual rounds of the seventh floor, when I happened by Mr. Bradford's room.

"Mrs. Mortensen, step away from Mr. Bradford and give me those scissors! Handles first. You've been warned time and time again to stop going into other peoples' rooms. Dr. Peterson told me to put you in lock-down if you did it, again. You got the scissors from my desk drawer, didn't you?"

"Then you should've kept it locked, Miss."

"Listen, do you need an escort to your room? Go now. Mr. Bradford, are you all right?"

"Oh, yes. I'm fine, thank you. I wasn't frightened in the least."

"I'll have to inform Dr. Peterson about this and he'll probably want to talk to both of you about this incident. He warned me that you two shouldn't even be talking to each other."

"Why is that?"

"I'll have him tell you."

evenge

ather 'round, children," I said, "I've got to tell you something important."

"It's story time!" one of them yelled and six pairs of ears perked up.

"It's not that kind of a story. You know that your brother, Jackie's been missing for two days and now I'm going to tell you what happened to him."

My ears lay flat as I choked back tears. "Remember when I rushed all of you back to our warren because the human was cutting his grass with that hellish, noise-making lawnmower? All of you, except little Jackie, made it safely home."

"What happened, Momma?" the children asked in unison.

"When I realized that Jackie wasn't with us, I went back out to find him and … he must've been hiding under a pine tree. I heard him screaming. The human ran over him with the lawnmower. There was nothing I could do to save him. Then, the human ran over him again and the screaming stopped. I watched helplessly as I saw bits of fur and flesh fly out of the mower."

The children and I started sobbing and I tried my best to console them. Then I told them that I had a plan for revenge against the savage human.

"Momma, can we help?"

"No, it'll be too dangerous."

At times like this, I wish their father was here to help me. I told the children that a cat had killed him, but the truth is that as soon as the children were born, the shit-heel hopped away from home.

Humans, unlike other predators, can kill their prey for sport, even kill each other and successfully and often unsuccessfully, justify their reasons for doing so.

I decided to seek out a predator, a killing machine, just as dangerous and crafty as a human. I asked a chicken hawk for a temporary truce. It landed on a low branch and grasped it tightly in its powerful talons. Eye-to-eye contact was difficult for me because I was looking into black, murderous eyes and any slight twitch I made, might be my last.

It leaned forward, wings flared. I stiffened in fear.

"What's in it for me?" it said.

"The humans who live here, have a little puppy dog. It seems to be as well-loved as a child and if anything happened to it, their hearts would be crushed."

"And you want me to swoop down and kill it?"

"Yes. It's a little poodle, probably weighs only about three pounds. Maybe if you flew high into the air and dropped it."

"I'll do it any way I want, rabbit!"

"Okay, okay. They let it outside every morning at sunrise. Sometimes, but not always, one of them comes out of the house with it."

"It doesn't make any difference to me whether they're present or not. They couldn't stop me anyway," it said in a low whisper which terrified me. "Tomorrow then. Be advised that our truce will be over and you and your young had better stay in your hole. And henceforth, remain watchful."

I shuddered as it flapped its wings gaining altitude, then glided on the wind currents. Remain watchful, it warned.

The next morning, a shriek and a painful scream woke me. I knew immediately what had happened. My family and I began making plans to move.

eaving

irst of all, I left home when I was nine. My name is Howard Langley.

I'd shared a one-room house with my parents and my older sister. Because I was the youngest child, my job was to make sure that our coal furnace was properly banked and always burning, through fall and winter nights. Sometimes, I was up all night keeping it lit.

It was 1946 and my parents didn't believe in owning gas appliances for fear of accidently blowing up our house. Water was heated on a woodstove for our baths. I had to wait for my dad and mom to finish their baths before taking mine. By that time, the water had already turned cold and murky. My twelve-year-old sister, Karen, prima donna that she was, heated water for her own bath. She had the only bedroom in the house. The bedroom was simply a bed and two curtains in the corner.

Karen was taking a bath. Up until the moment I saw two balled-up pairs of socks lying next to her bra on her bed, I had believed her to be extremely well-endowed for a twelve-year-old. It occurred to me that I should never tell her about it.

Both my parents rode the same streetcar to their jobs at the munitions plant. My dad had been declared 4-F by the draft board and therefore never served in the military. I knew it was because of his loss of three fingers while working at the plant; one on his left hand and two on his right.

My mom started working there in 1944. I believe it was to keep an eye on him, although I could never understand why. He had a disturbing array of moles and carbuncles which he tried, unsuccessfully, to conceal by growing a beard. My mom, on the other hand, had a flawless complexion. It was her only positive attribute. Her hair was always horribly matted. She stood four feet ten-and-a-half and had a dowager's hump. But, they were good people.

We ate beans three times a day. In addition to our coal furnace, it kept our mattresses warm on cold nights. I remember that my dad would make a ceremonious production of scooping the square, ham fat patty off the top of the beans and eating it first. My mom and sister would always laugh and clap their hands when he did this. I never understood why.

So, in June, coincidentally on the second anniversary of the D-day Invasion, I packed a cardboard suitcase with a few clothes, a razor and some shaving powder. I hadn't planned on ever coming back.

I set out to discover post-war America and perhaps, write a couple of folksongs.

Buchanan Elementary School, which I had formerly attended, was at the end of our block. In all of my nine years, I had never been anyplace other than the city block on which we lived. My parents tried to instill in me the value of staying in one place and settling down.

I began hitchhiking and wherever I landed, managed to find work doing odd jobs. Then, after a couple of weeks, or a month, I'd move on. I'd tell prospective employers I was thirteen and if they didn't believe me, I told them that my whole family was small for our ages.

On my way to turning ten, I had worked as a janitor, a dishwasher, a soda jerk and pumped gas. The gas station owner told me to always check a customer's oil while the engine was hot, so the dipstick would indicate that the oil level was low. Then he'd sell them a quart. When I hit the road again, I had reached Casper, Wyoming. Hitchhiking just outside of Casper, was when I met Bob. He roared up on an Indian motorcycle.

"My name's Bob. What's yours?"

"Folks call me, Howie."

"Glad to meetcha, Howie. How far ya goin'?"

"Probably as far as you're going."

"Well, I'm goin' as far as California. Are ya up to it?"

"I guess."

"I just came from a motorcycle rally in Sturgis."

"Sturgis? What's Sturgis?"

"A town in South Dakota. Every year they have a rally."

Bob told me that in the war, he was a Marine in the Pacific. He explained what it was like on Iwo Jima. He used the word, "bloodbath." I've always been glad that people like Bob, won the war for the rest of us.

We worked a little on the way to California and finally stopped at a place called Bakersfield. Bob said he intended to join a motorcycle club called the "Hell's Angels," who were looking for a few good men. Bob was accepted for membership and it was suggested that I become the club's mascot.

I was introduced to their leader, Blackie and his girlfriend, Doris. Blackie wore a patch over his right eye and Doris had a torn earlobe and her front teeth were missing. But, they were nice to me, as were all the club members.

Blackie and Doris adopted me and I lived with them in their Airstream, along with their dog, a Doberman-Shepherd mix.

When I turned twelve, they said that it was time I started riding with them. One guy named Lip, (I don't know why they called him that) told me I could ride on the back of his Harley. They'd often ride out on what they called, "missions" and drive for about sixty miles in whatever direction Blackie decided and returned after dark. To me, these missions didn't seem to serve any particular purpose. I did notice, however, that other motorists appeared terror-stricken. Maybe that was the point.

One day, Blackie called the club together saying that they were going on a very serious mission. He told Doris he was taking his "pal." I thought he meant me, but he was talking about his .45. I usually stayed home with Doris when the club went on serious missions. Doris later revealed to me that those kinds of missions were wars with rival clubs. Most of the club's members were World War Two veterans who had recently been in a war. It was hard for me to understand why they'd want to keep fighting wars.

Doris told Blackie that I should go to school. So, that fall, after my thirteenth birthday, I was enrolled in the fifth grade. My old friend, Bob, who had taken some college courses on the G.I. Bill, was enlisted to help me with my homework. After getting straight A's for the year, the school promoted me past sixth grade into seventh.

When I graduated from high school, the club decided unanimously that I would attend college. Stanford was their choice. The club, then embarked on extensive fund-raising missions. I was told not to go with them. They raised tens of thousands of dollars in donations from banks, businesses, armored truck companies and wealthy individuals. I gratefully accepted the money, with neither assumptions, nor questions.

And so, I went to Stanford and earned a B.A. in history. Not satisfied with that and because Stanford had an excellent Law School, I decided to pursue a Juris Doctorate. I told Blackie and Doris of my plan. They seemed genuinely pleased. The club enthusiastically resumed their fund-raising missions by visiting their usual sources.

Among the many donors was a very and quite surprisingly generous gift given by the Pagans, a rival motorcycle club. Each of my additional three years at Stanford, were paid for by the Hell's Angels annual fund-raising missions.

The FBI declared the club, my club, a crime organization. Blackie said it was a lie.

I graduated Stanford Law, Suma Cum Laude, with a J.D. and passed the Bar on my first attempt. Trial Law would become my career path. Blackie liked that idea.

I defended the Bakersfield chapter of the Hell's Angels pro bono, but charged the other chapters, as well as other clubs. The alleged crimes always varied from aggravated robbery to assault, to murder ... the usual things.

I won so many cases that I now have two walk-in closets full of Armani suits surrounded by a twelve-room house on three acres. I suppose the reason why I won most cases, is that the prosecutors had so much difficulty locating witnesses.

Many years have passed and the old club members have since died—Bob, Lip, Doris, Blackie and others whose names I've forgotten—all gone. They have my eternal gratitude for everything they've done for me and for everything I've become.

The present Bakersfield chapter and the other chapters' memberships are filled with common thieves, drug addicts and street punks. I no longer represent motorcycle clubs. These days I keep busy defending white-collar criminals.

I turned seventy-five last summer and some people, when they're older, like to go back home and visit their squalid origins ... curiosity, perhaps.

I flew back and found that my old neighborhood, the block and my childhood home had been demolished; replaced by senior citizen high-rises. In a rental car, I drove around for a while and then decided to visit the records division at the court house. I discovered that my old house had a gas explosion in the winter of 1948. Three people perished; my parents and sister. My sister, Karen, probably convinced my dad to enter the twentieth century and buy gas appliances. That was all I wanted to know. Thomas Wolfe was wrong when he said, "You can't go home." What he should've said was, "You shouldn't go home."

The following day, I took an afternoon flight back to Palm Springs and my wife, Lydia. Lydia was Lip's daughter by his second girlfriend.

nterim

s a retired pastor, I had myself placed on the ELCA's list of available interim ministers for churches in immediate need of a pastor while they seek a permanent one.

And so, I was called to a small Lutheran church in Wabasha, Minnesota. It was only an hour's drive from where I lived and I accepted the job.

I'd known that Wabasha had been the setting for the movie *Grumpy Old Men*. When I first arrived, I was told by my temporary congregants that none of the movie had been filmed there, except for a wide shot of the steeple at Saint Basil's Catholic Church.

In my capacity as an interim pastor, there had been some unusual circumstances in which I had to perform my duties, but this one I'd never experience before. Their minister had died and my first duty was to officiate at his funeral.

In preparation for delivering his eulogy, I asked a few of his family members and member of the church for information about him and his background. I was told that he loved a good joke, had a marvelous sense of humor and often infused humor into his sermons. But, when I asked the cause of his passing, some turned away and some burst into tears. He had committed suicide a year before his retirement. So, I had some questions to ask the funeral director.

The funeral director told me that he had the deceased fitted with a wig to cover the entrance and exit wounds caused by a large-caliber pistol. He further told me that the wig's color and density closely matched the Reverend's own hair. The funeral director was bald and I wondered if he had donated his own wig and before the casket was closed, he would quickly snatch it back.

Pastor Nyberg came to Saint Mark's Lutheran Church as a freshly ordained seminarian nearly forty-five years ago. He was dearly loved by all, until his wife found out that he was cheating on her with the church organist. Although the cheating went on for several years, it was recently discovered when the dead Reverend failed to delete the e-mails to and from his paramour. Apparently, they communicated, via e-mails, when and where in Lakeville they'd have their trysts. Technology, it could be said, played a part in his demise ... a large part.

The funeral director, it turned out, was the local gossip-monger. He filled me in on the latest news regarding the former pastor and the former organist. "Yeah, the three of them were adulterers." He said, gravely.

"Three?" I interjected.

"If I may use a hockey metaphor, it was a genuine hat-trick. The organist was cheating on her husband, her husband was cheating on her and Nyberg was cheating on his wife."

I countered with, "If Nyberg's wife was cheating on him at the same time and if I used a baseball metaphor, it could be called an adulterous grand slam.

"Oh, now you've gone a little too far, mister. I mean pastor."

I went back to my office, having been well-informed enough to deliver a proper eulogy. The funeral was set for Monday; visitation at 11:00, funeral at noon, burial, followed by a reception and lunch in the church basement.

I thought I'd use the Lazarus story or, the Lord's resurrection for starters.

Perhaps because of the recent sex scandal, there were only about twenty people attending the funeral, including his wife, children, their spouses and four grandchildren. I waited 'til everyone stopped coughing before I began.

Inasmuch as the deceased liked a joke, at the last minute, I decided to tell one: "A priest, a rabbi and a minister walk into a bar. All three suffered concussions." The mourners stared at me slack-jawed. They probably didn't get it, as most of them dumbly shook their heads.

With the sermon over, the procession to the gravesite was next. I had filled a small, glass vial with cigar ashes for the "ashes to ashes bit." No one would know.

The funeral director and I shared the lead car. He asked me to drive because he was still detoxifying. "You know that joke you told at the funeral? I thought it was highly inappropriate," he slurred.

After the graveside ceremony, I was approached by a very stern looking gentleman. By then, everyone looked stern. "You won't be welcomed at the reception. Stay away. In fact, stay away forever. Your deportment today was despicable and we've decided that your services are no longer required. Furthermore, we'll continue to look for another interim pastor, thank you very much."

It was only a slight inconvenience for me to pack up the things I had in my former office. I phoned my wife and told her that I would be home for dinner from now on. She didn't ask why. She already knew.

"So, what was it this time, Jimmy?"

"I told a joke."

"Big deal. You often tell jokes in your sermons."

"This was a funeral and it wasn't appreciated."

"Oh, well I can see why. Jimmy, what possesses you to say and do those things? Before you retired, you were kicked out of two churches."

"I was asked to resign."

"Same thing! At one church, you stood at the pulpit with a Bible and tore out pages from the 'Book of Leviticus,' saying it didn't belong. I mean, what the hell?"

"I only did it for dramatic effect. My sermon was all about intolerance."

"How about the time you decided to liven things up by changing the sacramental wine to Sangria. Then, before a wedding, drank a bottle of it and had to send an usher for another bottle

"You could barely stand for the ceremony. And you wonder why no one wants you."

"I can't help it that nobody likes style, anymore."

"I checked the mail today and you've got a letter from a church in La Crosse. I can't believe that word hasn't spread about your antics."

"Well, they may be progressive enough to appreciate my 'antics.' They might want to put a little oomph into their lives. You never know."

"That's the problem, you never know. I think you should quit altogether, now."

"Why, what else is there for me to do?"

"Clean the gutters."

nto thin air

ivorce was finalized. I knew this was coming and can't say I'm surprised. Bob, my husband, waited until our children were grown and moved out, plus he had just retired from his job as an electrician. Timing was always his forte. Did he ever cheat? I don't think so. He had a personality as dull as a hammer. Was he planning on, after forty years, seeing other women? Highly implausible. And I probably wouldn't be rejoining the dating scene either. We both had gained a lot of weight, even though he'd aged better than I.

According to the decree, we were to split joint bank accounts and jointly owned property. We would have an estate sale and sell off the furniture. Then came the sale of our house.

I came out of the divorce with more money because Bob, in his usual wisdom, had to spend a few thousand on a fancy lawyer. I, being a patent attorney, represented myself. It turned out to be an amicable dissolution. Diana Northrup, former wife of Bob Northrup, would be just fine. We'd both be fine. Bob, with social security and union pension and I, two years from retirement and armed with a lot of money stashed in a personal savings account at a bank known only to myself, would do okay.

I wanted to stay near work in Augusta and contacted the real estate agent we had used to sell our home.

The real estate agent, a Mr. Gary Comfrey, motioned me to a chair in front of his desk. His interest in selling me a home was genuine, but his northern Maine accent was affected and folksy. His hairdo was quite interesting; the receding hairline, in a few years, would eventually meet the bald spot at the top of his head. So, he slicked his dark hair straight back. If central casting was looking for a snake oil salesman, he'd get the part. But, his appearance had nothing to do with his warm, engaging personality.

"Well, Mrs. N. I'm sorry, I guess you're not a Missus anymore."

"It's all right, Gary. Perhaps you can just call me Diana."

"Ayyuh, it's Diana then. I've got a two-bedroom bungalow in Belgrade, a little over ten miles away right up Augusta Road. It useta be a summah cabin, but we've upgraded for yeah-round. Everything up to code, ayyuh."

"Belgrade, where the population doubles in the summer?"

"More like triples."

He pushed a picture of the house across his desk.

"I'm interested in seeing it, Gary. How much is it?"

He looked at the picture and fidgeted. "The list price is $200,099."

"I'll give you $190,000, cash."

"All right, then. Let's take my cah. First, I want to disclose somethin' about the house. Ya know, in case ya change ya mind."

"What's wrong with it?"

"Nothin' wrong a'course. It was the summah home of Joseph Force Crater. *Judge* Crater."

"Oh, he's the big-time judge who disappeared?"

"Ayyuh, the same and some folks believe the place is haunted."

"Even if it was, it still wouldn't dissuade me from buying it."

He insisted on telling me more about Judge Crater.

"Crater was a New York City judge who vanished, poof, on the night of August 6, 1930."

I interrupted, "Maybe he took a plane ride with Amelia Earhart."

He didn't seem to like my interrupting his story, sighed deeply and continued.

"It was rumored that he, acting as official receiver in a bankruptcy, sold a property at a fraction of the three million bucks the city paid to get it back. So, the judge made a huge profit which lead to wide-spread speculation that he was murdered in a dispute about the money. In another account of his disappearance, it was well-known that he was very close friends with Broadway showgirls and prostitutes who were mixed up with the Mob and that meant trouble for him."

"Do you think someone kidnapped him?" I felt compelled to ask.

"There was no ransom note. No phone call about a ransom. Maybe a botched kidnapping, or his wife found out about the girlfriends and hired somebody to kill him. Anyway, he was last seen leaving a restaurant on West 45th Street wearing a linen suit and a straw, Panama hat. I guess it was a hot day in the city."

"Gary, this Judge Crater thing seems like it's become an obsession with you."

"It's only a history of the house. Thought ya might liketa know. Ayyuh, it's all in the abstract."

We drove up and looked at the house that would be my permanent home. Gary explained that it was previously used as a summer rental in the resort town. For a home that was over eighty-years old, it was beautifully refurbished. The only problem I saw, was one of the bedrooms was too small for anything except a TV room or a library. The other bedroom was large enough to fit a queen-sized bed.

On the way back to his office, I asked Gary if Bob was using him as his Realtor. He said that he was, but couldn't tell me where Bob was going to live. He assured me it wasn't anywhere near Belgrade.

I hesitated to ask him any more about Judge Crater, but did anyway. "What happened with his wife?"

"Funny how they met; Crater was his future wife's divorce lawyer. Her name was Stella. Well, after he disappeared, she didn't want to stay in Belgrade, so she moved back into the couple's Fifth Avenue apartment and was evicted when she couldn't pay the rent."

"Didn't he leave her any money?"

"It wasn't 'til 1939 that she had him declared legally dead after all efforts to find him were exhausted. Then and only then, could she collect on his life insurance. Stella was back in the bucks, ayyuh."

"Was it a lot?"

"Back in those days, it was."

"Gary, I'll sign the papers and write you a check. By the way, don't tell Bob where I'm going."

The deal was set to close two weeks later. Gary accompanied me on the final walk through prior to closing.

"Gary, how come the floor sounds hollow when we walk on it?"

"That's 'cause it is hollow. The house is sitting on three courses of cement blocks. Ayyuh, it's because it's so close to the lake. Wouldn't want ya to get flooded."

I checked out of the hotel in Augusta. The furnishings I'd bought were in storage and planned to meet the movers in Belgrade.

After the movers left, I decided to take a short nap and then sample the nightlife in downtown Belgrade.

Driving a short distance, I found the business district and a nice bar and restaurant; ate and had a couple of martinis. Maybe it was three or four. After all, it was a Saturday night.

It was 11:15 when I got home and went straight to bed. Gary had been guilty of filling my head with that Judge Crater nonsense that I thought I'd have difficulty falling asleep. But, fell asleep right away.

I wakened to someone knocking on the front door. I threw on a white, terrycloth robe which I don't remember owning. It was daylight and a hazy, morning sun shone through the front window. When I opened the door a man about forty years-old, dressed in a cream-colored linen suit and a straw Panama hat, smoking a cigar and holding out a coffee cup, softly said, "Hi, I'm your neighbor. Name's Joe and I was wondering if I could borrow a cup of sugar?"

I hardly ever panic, but I slammed the door, turned the deadbolt and ran back to the bedroom.

I sat up in bed. My nightgown was drenched in vodka sweat and my hair was plastered to my face. The nightstand clock read 3:35 a.m. I was still shaking even though I realized it was a nightmare. It's silly, but I went out to the living room to check and see if I *had* locked the door. It was locked, but I still had an uneasy feeling and didn't know if I could get back to sleep.

I made a pot of coffee and wanted, after all the excitement, to read the most boring book on my bookshelf and picked out the inert biography of Calvin Coolidge. This would most certainly put me in la-la land.

Came the dawn and Calvin hadn't done what I'd hoped. Of course, the coffee hadn't helped. I opened the door to check the weather and on the top step was a coffee cup. Trying to stifle the scream rising in my throat, I raised my hand to my mouth. Too late. I screamed through my fingers, inhaled and screamed again.

hen the hazmat-suited NTSB investigators arrived at the crash site of a Boeing 757, they began pawing through the wreckage of twisted metal and found the cockpit flight recorder; AKA, the black box. The black box wasn't black; more like the orange of a traffic cone.

They listened to the playback's final words: "Ahhh, this is your Captain ..." calmly, at first. "We've lost power in both engines ..." Then, more urgently, "Trying to restart ... (expletive) ... (unintelligible) ..." Shouting, "We're going down!" Followed by the *shhh* of white noise.

The aircraft lay in several pieces scattered over a Pennsylvania farmer's fallow field. The fuselage was split in half and the wings were an acre apart with the engines only partially attached.

The investigators had determined that there was no explosion or fire. Some passengers were found in the aft section of the plane, still strapped in. They were as dead as the passengers who were thrown clear of the plane and into the field.

There were ninety-seven passengers plus five crewmembers. None survived. But, only ninety-six bodies of the passengers were found. A recount was ordered. Five crewmembers and ninety-six passengers. The number remained the same. Then, the passenger manifest was examined. Evidently, ninety-seven passengers boarded.

After the dead were identified, a man named Michael Haskins, while listed on the manifest, was not found in the identification process. They found Seat D 29 to which he had been assigned. He had boarded at Harrisburg, Pennsylvania and was supposed to have flown non-stop bound for Pawtucket, Rhode Island. They did, however, find his luggage.

ike Haskins was drafted after high school by the Boston Red Sox organization and sent to play for their double-A team, the

SeaDogs, in Portland, Maine. At eighteen, he was playing as a professional, a game that he loved more than anything. In high school, he also played football as a running back and college scouts were giving him a look. But, baseball won out because Mike realized that he could have a longer career in a sport where injuries were less common and less severe.

"Keep on callin' yerself Mike," a teammate counseled. "You don't wanna call yerself Mickey or Mick. Not in this game and I think you know why."

He knew. Anyone who'd seen Mickey Mantle play or even remotely heard of him, knew why. But, the manager and coaches couldn't help make comparisons. At five-eleven and one-hundred-ninety pounds, not only was he built like *The Mick*, he had speed on the base paths, power at the plate as well as speed in center field where he could rob a batter of a double or triple.

In July of his second season with the Sea Dogs, Mike's manager took him to one side after a road game with the Harrisburg Senators.

"Mike, you've got tremendous talent, the fans love you, your teammates love you, but I'm gonna hate to let you go."

"What? Why, Skip? I thought I was doin' pretty good!"

"You are, Mike. Lemme finish. You've been called up to triple-A and they want you there in two days. You're gonna by playin' for the Paw Sox in Rhode Island. After that ... the Red Sox! Who knows? I know that the Red Sox are always lookin' for talent. Not just a good glove, but somebody who brings a lot of lumber to the plate. I got a feelin' you'll be playin' in the Bigs before too long"

"Gee, Skip, can't I at least finish out this series with the Senators?"

"With the way they're playin'? We can sweep 'em with or without you. They sent you a plane ticket and cab fare. Then, when you land in Rhode Island, take a cab to Days Inn and as soon as you check in, call Daryl Anderson. He's the Paw Sox manager."

"I don't know what to say."

"Don't say anything, just go."

Mike Haskins settled into his seat on the plane and put any thoughts away with regard to playing centerfield for the Red Sox at Fenway. He didn't want to jinx himself. Furthermore, he was glad it was the Sox and not the Yankees. The Yankees with their short-haired corporate look, played their games with a joylessness not seen anywhere else. It was well-known that they lured the best players from other teams with seven, eight-figure salaries and had the payroll to do it. *Stop thinking about it!* he scolded himself.

Seated next to him at the window seat, was an older woman, about forty. They had begun to make small-talk, when the Captain interrupted with the announcement that he had lost control and the plane was going down. The woman began to scream. Everyone started to scream. Mike cinched his seatbelt tighter, bent over and put his hands over his ears to muffle the screams. Men who shouted deep-throated, now were screaming in higher, shriller pitches. The aircraft immediately lost altitude and went spinning in lazy freefall.

When the plane slammed into the ground, passenger Michael Haskins was not on board.

"Phil, this is Daryl. Your boy, Haskins isn't here. Should've been here by now. I called the hotel and he didn't check in. What the hell's going on?"

"You didn't hear what happened? He was on the plane that went down."

"Ah Jesus, Phil! I'm sorry."

Still with hands clamped over his ears, jaw clenched, eyes tightly closed, he felt a mild breeze and the warmth of the sun across his body. Mike neither had fallen asleep, nor had been unconscious. The last thing he remembered was being aware of the plane falling. The flashes of sunlight through the cabin windows meant that it was spinning. He couldn't hear screaming anymore, took his hands from his ears and opened his eyes. Lying face down on a hard-packed dirt path or narrow road, he raised his head and saw tall grass and taller weeds along the roadside.

His mother had told him, "When dead people first arrive in heaven, they don't know what happened and they're confused, but then, they get it." And she added, "They don't feel pain anymore."

Pain. He didn't feel pain. Had he been thrown from the crash from a great height or just a few feet? It didn't matter. There would be injuries. Always a ballplayer's fears that he'd wind up on the disabled list for weeks or months or an entire season and be replaced by somebody else coming up from double-A. Mike began an inventory of his body parts. His vision was clear. No concussion. No neck injury. Hands, arms and shoulders were fine. Ribcage, pelvis, legs and ankles were okay. Relieved that his spinal cord wasn't severed, he wouldn't be seeing himself in a wheelchair for the rest of his life when, in old-age, he'd be regaling youngsters of his grand two-year baseball career.

Confused by where he actually was. Was he dead and his mangled body found in the wreckage on a field in Pennsylvania? Was he in purgatory where he'd have to gain points to enter heaven or lose points and go the hell? Maybe he was caught up in The Rapture? Mike's mother had instilled in him common sense and level-headedness. She also taught him to believe in whatever he wanted to believe and, of course, to have enough sense to "pound sand in a rat hole." As a result of logic and reasoning, he didn't believe in The Rapture and people who believed in it were so afraid of death that they figured this was a way to avoid it. But, their bodies were always found and put into the ground or cremated. All right, he thought, he was alive, but that still didn't answer questions with regard to where he was or how he got there.

He thought of his girlfriend, Becky and how she was going to meet him in Pawtucket, but hearing that he was missing from his flight, she'd probably call his parents in Nebraska and together they'd do everything they could to locate him. Mike knew that they'd be worried and upset. He imagined his father calling their congressman and demanding answers.

As he watched the southwesterly arc of the sun, he thought back to the chain of events which brought him to this place, wherever this place was. The day game had ended at three-thirty. He had showered and went back to the team's hotel to pack the few clothes he'd brought with him to Harrisburg including his glove and a baseball. Then, caught a cab and arrived at the airport at five. The flight departed at seven-o-three. And it was now, he looked at his watch, seven-thirty-five. Were the flight successful, he would've landed in Rhode Island at around eight.

Mike rolled over onto his back, sat, pulled his knees up and leaned back on his hands. He felt the urge to start walking northeast toward Rhode Island and he'd better start doing it before nightfall.

Looking east at the curving road, he spotted flashing strobe lights on the horizon. Was it merely a mirage? It, whatever it was, hurtled toward him, then slowed as it got nearer. Red, white and blue lights ablaze in a non-synchronous frenzy. *Three cheers for the red, white and blue!* Mike sat forward with his forearms on his knees, waiting for whatever happened next.

It looked like an all-black cop car except that it was a coup with a bubble-top. The lights, instead of being attached, were embedded into the car and ran from the top down the sides of the doors like a horseshoe. Both gull-wing doors opened and out stepped what Mike assumed to be a police officer.

The figure, obviously a tall, slim woman in a form-fitting black uniform, walked purposefully in his direction. She also wore a silver-colored helmet with a black, tinted, full-face visor and knee-high boots. She stood in front of him, hands on hips. A voice, without inflection stated, "Are you able to stand."

"Oh, sure," Mike said and started to rise. The officer extended a gloved right hand, he reached for it, but she took hold of his wrist and slipped her other hand on the underside of his elbow. *Hey, be careful, that's my throwing arm.*

With fluid ease, she pulled him to his feet. They both stepped back a pace. *Who is this woman?* Mike asked himself. *She's gotta be at least six-five and holy shit, she's strong as a bull!* He smoothed a dark forelock from his brow and massaged the back of his neck where he felt a knot developing. Above her left breast, he read a white, printed semi-circled, POLICE and below it, a badge embroidered in silver thread. Nothing much ever frightened Mike Haskins, but he had to admit that he was just a little scared of what seemed to be the unknown … waiting for him.

He was relieved to see that this police officer wasn't wearing anything on her belt; no pepper spray, no handcuffs, no nightstick and, most importantly, no sidearm.

"Are you all right." She said it not like a question, but as a statement.

"Yeah, I'm okay."

"Do you have any identification papers." Again, a flat statement.

"I've got my driver's license. Here, I'll take it out of my wallet."

Before she took it, she asked, "How did you get here."

"My car stalled back there." He pointed behind him with his thumb. "I got tired of walking and sat down."

It was a lie and he could almost hear his mother say, "If you tell one lie, you have to tell another and another and another." He felt that he couldn't, shouldn't tell that he survived a plane crash.

"You have a car."

"Yes. I think it ran out of gas." He held out his license and she studied it from behind her visor.

"A car with gas in it," she said. "This is a Maine driver's license."

"That's right. I live in Maine."

"How old are you."

"Twenty and I've got 'til next year to renew it."

"Yes, it expires in 2017. Do you know where you are."

"I was hoping you'd tell me."

"The outskirts of New York City."

Though this police officer presented no danger to Mike, he was afraid of what she could do to him. His fear anxiety and imagination were all in play. When she handed his license back, Mike thought briefly of attacking her and catching her by surprise, but reasoned that a well-placed kick to his groin would probably launch his testicles into his throat, even if he was wearing a cup. He was also at a disadvantage not knowing her expression, especially her eyes behind her dark visor. Was she smiling? Was she wide-eyed? Was one eyebrow arched? Maybe she didn't have eyebrows and had cameras for eyes and was probably not even human: NYPD's new secret weapon.

Maybe she was an android like Commander Data on *Star Trek*.

She was looking toward him when she spoke, not too him, but to someone else, "He's clear, but I would advise a medical evaluation. He's too well-dressed to be one of them."

Well-dressed? It's just a navy-blue polo shirt, tan khaki pants and white tennies. One of them?

Then to Mike, "We have to leave now. A group of Outlanders are coming this way."

"Outlanders? Are you arresting me?"

"No. Get into the car. Hurry."

The car was a two-seater. No backseat. As soon as he took his place beside the non-human, both doors closed. One seatbelt automatically wrapped around one shoulder and another, surprising him, pinned his upper torso to the backrest. Both belts clicked into place. With no steering wheel, it looked like one of those newly invented driverless cars.

"Start," she said. "Reverse course."

The car made a buzzing sound as it made a tight U-turn.

"Increase speed to eighty."

Mike was concerned with the bubble car going eighty because he felt that he probably wouldn't survive another crash.

The bubble car sped along on straightaways and automatically slowed on curves.

"I have to ask you a question," she said without turning her helmet toward Mike.

"Go ahead." He felt a clamminess crawling over himself. He was apprehensive and didn't know what her question would be or what answer she might've wanted to hear.

"Where were you going when I picked you up."

"Rhode Island. I'm going to start a new job there."

"Rhode Island," she said from her unseen mouth, or her wherever.

Mike swore to himself that he could actually hear her positronic brain whirring through its connections.

"There's no Rhode Island. If there ever was, it's not on the map, now."

She's using contractions! She's been doing it all along! Commander Data didn't either, and that's how you could tell if it was his evil twin, Lore, because Lore did use contractions. But then again, she was probably programmed that way.

"I've got another question."

105

Mike was getting weary of the curveballs she was throwing at him.

"How did you get from Maine to Pennsylvania."

"On the team bus. How do you think we got there?"

"Team bus. What team."

"I'm a professional baseball player."

Now, it was time for him to throw curves. "Why wasn't someone dispatched from Philadelphia? It's closer."

This caught her attention. She turned her helmeted head in his direction. "Philadelphia is farther south than New York."

"I left Harrisburg an hour ago ... wait. Is Harrisburg ... does Harrisburg exist anymore?"

"Harrisburg doesn't exist."

"Why not?" He was hoping that her computerized brain would overload and explode. "How many cities are there in Pennsylvania?"

"Two. Philadelphia and Pittsburgh."

He couldn't believe it, but as he gazed around at all the vacant landscape, he began to believe that he landed in an entirely different world. Not Maine, not Pennsylvania and definitely not Kansas. He didn't see one single tree, only a few stumps. Tall grass was flattened in several places.

He threw her another curve: "Joe Biden's hometown is Scranton, Pennsylvania. Is there a Scranton?"

There's no Scranton. Who's Joe Biden."

"Just the V-POTUS, that's all."

"V-POTUS. I don't understand."

You don't understand something, he thought. *Join the not understanding anything club, baby.*

"The Vice President, for godssake!"

"I don't know him."

With his curveballs, Mike had her swinging like a rusty gate. Little Leaguers usually shouted the simile at opposing batters.

"Why don't you know him? Have you ever heard of him?"

"No."

"Okay," he laughed, "in all fairness, most people don't remember vice presidents unless they become president, like Truman, LBJ and daddy Bush and nobody remembers the losing vice-presidential candidates."

As the car began slowing, she said, "I still don't know what you're talking about."

Mike saw, as they approached what appeared to be their destination, two tall, thick, steel doors which looked like a gate of some sort, but there were no walls. He could see people and buildings beyond it. The car pulled up short of the gate, she got out, peeled off her left glove and placed her thumb on an access reader. *Why would they bother to put a thumbprint on an android?* The door on the right side slowly opened inward on tracks embedded in the ground. *What fresh hell is this?*

The car pulled up to the curb in front of a gray, stone building. A sign in large, block letters read: NY POLICE HEADQUARTERS. Gawking pedestrians were looking at the passenger and were perhaps wondering if Mike was a dangerous criminal or worse, an Outlander.

Standing in front of the building, a short, stocky man rocked on his heels. At first, he seemed impatient, but a grin crossed his face.

"This is Dr. Sorenson," Mike's driver said, robotically, "he's going to give you a medical evaluation."

The doctor thrust out his hand. Mike took it as they watched the android take her leave and drive the car around the corner.

"Hello, Mike. I'm glad to meet you." *He seems sincere, and real.*

"Let's go inside," Sorenson said, "it's getting quite humid out here."

They walked down a wide hallway where cops, male and female were gathered. They wore the same black, form-fitting uniforms as did the woman cop who'd picked him up. And they had the same silver helmets with the black, face visor. Some were holding the helmets in their hands, while others held them in the crooks of their arms. They gave Mike a quick glance and continued talking amongst themselves. They looked human.

"They're going to get briefed before they go on shift," Sorenson offered.

"Could I ask you about the officer who brought me in? Is she human?"

Turning down a narrower hallway, the doctor paused, putting one hand on the wall and bending over, clasping an arm across his ample stomach. "You mean Iris?" he laughed, "we always tell her that she acts like a robot and it's funny that you think she is."

"Android," Mike corrected.

This was followed by renewed gales of laughter which caused Sorenson to nearly lose his balance. Wiping his eyes with a knuckle, the doctor assured that she was, indeed human and that she acted completely human when she wasn't on duty. "Do you want to meet her sometime when she's off duty?"

No, not really."

"Let's talk in my office."

"Talk? I thought you were going to give me a medical exam."

I'm not that kind of a doctor. I'm the kind of doctor who doesn't get his hands dirty. You know, one of the police department's psychiatrists."

"I'm not crazy!"

"And I'm not saying you are. Have a seat." He motioned to a chair in front of his desk and sank into a faux leather, swivel chair. He leaned back and laced his fingers across his stomach. "I know there must be a firestorm going on inside your head right now, so why don't you just take a couple of moments and try to gather your thoughts?"

"How did I get here and who or what are the Outlanders?"

"I'll give you the answer to the one I know. The Outlanders are miscreants. More specifically, anarchists. They don't want to obey any laws at any level of government. There were two original factions, each wanting to lead a revolution. They fought against each other—hundreds were killed. So, realizing their folly, these anarchists banded together and began attacking our cities declaring civil war."

"Civil war? What happened then?"

"We launched a counterattack from a couple of our joint military bases. What could've last only a week, we made the war last a month, in hopes they would come to their senses. That was thirty years ago and even though their population has greatly diminished, we still try to stay alert."

"But, how did I get here? And how do I get to where I was going?"

"I wish I could give you some answers, but I can't. Evidently this wasn't your destination."

"What keeps the Outlanders out?"

"An electrified force-field. When anyone comes in contact with it, they get a shock, rendering them unconscious. Then, an officer picks them up and brings them about ten miles away. Leaving them out in the middle of nowhere always leads to confusion."

"Is that what happened to me?"

Dr. Sorenson rolled his eyes toward the ceiling, then sat forward looking at Mike. "No, not at all."

"How do you know that I'm not an Outlander?"

"Your clothes, clean-shaven, recent haircut. All those things. Anyway, where did you get those clothes? They look strange."

The doctor's clothes looked strange to Mike, as well. His gray suitcoat had no lapels and it only came to his beltline. He wore a white shirt, buttoned at the top, with no tie. Odd that his shirt also had not collar.

"Tell me, Mike, what was the last thing you remember doing, before Iris found you sitting on the ground?"

"I got on an airplane. It crashed. I thought it crashed."

"Wait a minute. You told Iris you drove your car, that it broke down and you had to walk. We have a video and audio record of it. Here it is."

A thin monitor rose out of the top of Sorenson's desk showing Haskins making that statement.

"The entire thing, from your first encounter with Iris, until I met you at the curb was being recorded. You see, all our officers have cameras and metal detectors in their helmets. So, it showed you weren't armed and therefore, posed no threat. Outlanders are usually armed with some king of weapon.

"Mike, we have neither privately owned vehicles, nor large passenger aircraft."

"How do people get around?"

"Public transportation," Dr. Sorenson leaned forward, elbows on his desk, fingers tented, gravely serious. "That's two lies, Mike. What really happened to you?"

"I don't know!"

"Well, I don't know either. This is real, not some bad dream you're having when you wake up in a cold sweat, breathing hard."

"I wish it was just a dream, Doc. I mean, Doctor. This is a mess. I only want to get to Pawtucket, Rhode Island to play baseball. I'm destined to someday play for the Red Sox."

"Perhaps you were destined to die in a plane crash."

"No, I'm moving up in the Red Sox farm system."

"Farm system? There is no farm system," Sorenson said, his frustration and impatience was beginning to show. He ran his fingers through his short, blond hair.

Mike was getting frustrated, too. "I remember being on a plane. I don't know how I survived and I don't know how I wound up here!"

"According to your driver's license—and I believe that you once owned a car—the expiration date was 2017. Do you know what month this is?"

"Yeah, July."

"What year do you think this is?"

Haskins knew a loaded question when he heard one. Sudden fear gripped him. "2016," he murmured.

"Did the plane you were on fly beyond the stratosphere? Did it get sucked up in the vortex of a black hole and deposit only you in an alternate universe? Einstein said time is fluid. But, then he said that the past, present and future existing simultaneously, is only an illusion. It was just a theory. On the other hand, you have Hawking saying that time travel is impossible. How you got here, we may never know."

"Where is here?" Mike asked, afraid of the answer.

"2158," the doctor said, casually.

"2158? Holy shit!"

"Yes, and in 2023, your parents probably declared you legally dead. But, there'd be a silver lining in all of it. They could collect on your life insurance."

Mike's jaw dropped. "I'm alive in this time, but dead in the past!"

"Listen, my young friend, everyone you've ever known in your life is long dead. And since you had no progeny, you're all alone. You have to start your life all over again."

Dr. Sorenson told Mike that while they were talking, he checked the Red Sox rosters from 2016 to present and found no evidence of any Mike Haskins having ever played for Boston.

"I hate to tell you this, Mike, but your timeline was destroyed somehow. However, since you play baseball, I can arrange a tryout for you with the Yankees."

"The Yankees? No, never!"

Getting angry, the doctor nearly shouted, "Then I'll have you locked up. You'll be studied as a scientific curiosity for the rest of your life. The Yankees are on the road in Chicago. They're due back tomorrow for a three-game homestand. Take the offer of a tryout or consider the alternative."

"If there's no air travel, how do teams travel to road games?"

"Only our sports teams fly. Each team has their own small jet. To minimize sabotage from the Outlanders—some of them may still have explosives—they can take off and land vertically."

Sorenson offered to take Mike on a tour of Yankee stadium. To Mike's chagrin, he saw that the stadium didn't remotely resemble the House that Ruth Built. It had much smaller dimensions. There was still the familiar white, picket façade beyond the outfield wall. He noticed too, that the infield was skinned, and the distances from home plate, plainly marked, were only three-hundred feet to center and two-hundred seventy-five feet down the lines. Softball dimensions. They played softball! Seven inning games, ten on each team, including four outfielders.

Mike easily made the team as a left-center fielder and wasn't entirely surprised that he had three women teammates; first base, catcher and a relief pitcher.

He had asked the manager why there was only one league and was told that the smaller markets dissolved.

The New York Yankees and their star player, Mike Haskins, boarded the team jet which would take them to their next road game in Pittsburgh. The manager went over the starting lineup. They had played the Pirates back in May and after dissecting the videos, discussed their weaknesses and strengths.

Three Outlanders hunched over a small, heat-seeking missile devise. As soon as the jet cleared the force field, one of them pushed a button to launch it.

First, an orange fireball in the mid-afternoon sky, then parts of the aircraft came fluttering down like decomposing leaves.

indication

There's a nightmare more terrifying than a visual and that's an auditory one that issues from an unconscious imagination. But, in my case, this is no nightmare. It's actually a memory.

It's a sound that wakes me from a fitful sleep. The rats! I can still hear them after nearly sixty years, the rats, with their squealing, chirping and hissing. If that wasn't bad enough, the foxes, coyotes and stray dogs, growling, barking, yipping, gnashing their teeth at each other. Fully awake, it's impossible to get back to sleep.

Nothing noteworthy ever happened in the small, farming community of Earl, Wisconsin, but on Thursday, November first, 1934, the *Spooner Advocate* ran the headline: NO TRACE OF MISSING GIRL. Sixteen-year old Lorraine LaFond had been abducted from her home on Sunday, October fourteenth by twenty-five-year-old, Carl Wilkins, a parolee of Waupun State Prison. He had served seven of a ten-year sentence for receiving stolen property. Lorraine and Carl were my parents. My name is Bill Wilkins.

The story of my mother's abduction, even though it had occurred before I was born, was told to me many times by my two older sisters, older brother and corroborated by my mother.

My dad, Carl Wilkins was a frequent visitor at the LaFond household, so it wasn't unusual that he stopped by on that Sunday morning in October. Sometimes he'd be invited to stay for dinner and he always accepted just to be near my mother. He'd hold her hand under the table. Other than Mom and Carl, there was her brother, fourteen-year old Bobby, who was my uncle and my grandma, Ruth. She had been widowed for eleven years since my grandpa Isaac was kicked in the head by a mule. Dad came over with his shotgun, killed the beast and stayed for dinner. Grandma didn't care much for Dad's looks especially when he didn't like what somebody said. His face would turn from mildly pleasant to a glowering, hateful and dangerously sinister glare. I'd heard that women sometimes enjoyed the company of men who were wound tight and living close to the edge.

He stood at the front door cradling the same shotgun in his arms that he used to kill the mule. Mom opened the door. "C'mon in, Carl."

"I just came over ta see if Bobby wanted to go huntin' with me. Where's your ma?"

"She's in the barn, milking. Bobby, do you wanna go hunting with Carl?"

"You bet! I'll be ready in a minute." Bobby went to his bedroom to get a jacket.

"Hurry up, Lorraine, before your ma comes back ta the house."

"Where are we goin'?"

"You'll see. Let's go."

"But, what about Bobby?"

"Screw 'im."

As they headed away from the house, Bobby came running out. "Hey, you guys, wait for me!"

My dad, not pointed, but waved the shotgun toward Bobby. "Get back in the house!"

Uncle Bobby followed them from a distance, then ran to the barn. "Ma, he took Lorraine!"

"What're you talkin' about? Who took her?"

"Carl! He had his shotgun! They were walkin' toward the river!"

"Godammit! I never should've trusted that man! I got two more cows that need to be milked and if I don't do it now, it'll be bad for 'em! Run to the house and call the police! Hurry!"

The Washburn County Deputy Sheriff who responded to the call, was surprised that Bobby and Grandma knew the identity of my mother's abductor. In fact, they described him thusly: "five-feet nine, one-hundred sixty-five pounds, dark complexioned, brown eyes, dark hair and wearing a wool, black and red plaid shirt with a matching cap and carrying a 12-gauge shotgun."

"Did she go with him, unwillingly?" the deputy asked.

"It sure looked like it," Bobby said. "He took her by the arm. Looked like he was pullin' her."

"I followed the path they took," Grandma said, her voice quavering, "but couldn't find a trace."

"I'll go back to H.Q. and we'll organize a search party."

Sheriff O'Dell, several deputies and a posse of citizens from Earl and Shell Lake began searching along the Namekagon riverbank, the direction where my future parents were last seen. No trace of them. Just like Grandma said. A rowboat belonging to Mr. Milo Butz, which had been tied to a tree at the riverbank, was reported missing. So, it was presumed that my mom and dad took it and either crossed the river or went up or downstream. The search party couldn't find the boat.

Searches and radio broadcasts were made every day for almost a month, to no avail. The case of the missing girl remained unsolved until the second week of November.

Mom sat in the back of the boat while Dad rowed upstream, shotgun propped beside him. The flatwater Namekagon was lined with old and young aspen, birch, oak, maple trees and stands of tall pine and spruce. Mom saw a fawn running through the woods, but Dad didn't look. He kept his eyes on her the entire time. About a mile later, they reached their destination: a small, dark shack on the shore, which my dad shared with his father. Since being paroled from Waupun, he had no other place to go.

"You live here?"

"Yeah, so what?" Dad answered as he tied the boat to a tree. "My old man's here. He's been wantin' ta meet ya."

Almost every day, the two men took turns raping her, getting drunk and sleeping. The shotgun was always kept at arm's length.

In the early dawn of November eighth, she grabbed the shotgun and made her escape while the men were either sleeping or passed out. It was hard to tell which. She had thought about taking the boat, but decided that she could move faster on foot. And it was only about a mile. So, she leaned the gun against the boat and started walking. She had to be careful not to cross paths with bears and bobcats that were known to prowl the woods. Being mauled be the animals in the woods couldn't be much worse than the animals in the shack. She should've brought the gun with her.

A light snow began to fall when the barn was in sight. She sprinted to the door, flung it open and shouted, "Ma!" Ma wasn't there, so she ran the ninety feet to the front door and found Grandma and Bobby sitting in the living room. Grandma stood, face florid, stalking toward my mother. "You little tramp! How could you run away with that man? He's gotta be twice your age!" Before Mom could say anything, Grandma slapped her hard enough to leave red finger marks on her pale cheek.

"Ma," Bobby said, "she didn't run away!"

"Shut the hell up, Bobby, or I'll hit you too!"

"Ma, will you listen? I was kidnapped and they, they raped me!"

"Grandma slapped her again before the sting and the marks had faded from the first slap.

"There's a place for you in Shell Lake, they call it a Home for Wayward Girls, and you're goin' there soon's I call the Sheriff."

"Lorraine, it's the same as a jail!" Bobby yelled and Grandma turned her attention to him and pounced, boxing him on the ears.

A deputy drove my mom to the county courthouse in Shell Lake and ushered her into a small conference room. Taking her statement: "Miss LaFond, you're implicating your boyfriend in your abduction."

"He's not my boyfriend!"

"Be that as it may. You also say that Carl Wilkins and his father, Dean Wilkins repeatedly raped you almost every day for four weeks. Is this true as you have stated?"

"Yes."

"Well, then those men are in very serious trouble. We found out that Carl's on parole and this violation could send him back to Waupun for a very long time." The deputy was looking for a reaction, but received none, just a cold stare right back at him.

"I'll have your statement typed up. Then I'll give it to the judge for your hearing."

"Why do I have to have a hearing?"

"Because your mother said that you might've enticed Carl."

"I did not entice him!" she hissed.

"Then the hearing's based on your opinion versus your mother's. I'll drive you to the Saint Anthony of Padua Home for Wayward Girls. It's only a few blocks away. And I'll try to push it through, so it should only take about three days. Listen, it won't be so bad."

"By the way, right now deputies are on their way to arrest Carl and his father."

Dad rolled over and saw that Mom wasn't there and neither was the shotgun.

"What the hell?" He stepped outside and the early afternoon sun stung his watery eyes. Snow fluttered down when the sun slipped behind a cloud. "I gotta stop the bitch!" He saw the boat and the gun leaning against it. Thought he'd take the boat and look for her, but didn't know how much of a head start she had.

"Carl Wilkins!" a voice thundered, "get away from that boat and walk toward us with your hands up!" Two bulky deputies stood in front of him, pistols drawn. A third deputy circled around to the door of the shack and strongly urged Dean Wilkins to come out, hands high.

"Put some pants on, Wilkins." The older man, looking like a trapped animal, complied and pulled on greasy bib overalls over a grimy t-shirt. Dean Wilkins stooped to pick up a pint bottle with a little bit of whiskey in it. "Leave it there and come out," the deputy said.

"Both of you are under arrest for abducting a girl against her will. A minor, at that."

"Let my dad go," Carl pleaded, "he had nothin' to do with it."

"That's what you say. You both held her captive."

My dad had talked to the public defender for the court case which was certainly going to happen. The lawyer advised him to enter a plea of guilty and "take his lumps like a man." The same lawyer paid a visit to Mom just before her hearing began. He told her that he could halt the hearing if she would drop the charges against my dad and his father. The lawyer reasoned that a forty-year sentence for the younger man and a thirty-year for the older would, in no way, rehabilitate either of them and, he added,

"Justice would not be well-served. Even though Carl was convicted on only one felony, he has an extensive record of felony arrests. Besides that, your dalliance with him, outside of marriage, is legally considered prostitution."

There was neither a hearing, nor a trial. My dad was free to go. So, he decided to visit my mother at the Home for Wayward Girls. Mom had thought long and hard about telling one of the nuns of Dad's parole violation and that would really fix his ass. Instead, she decided to bide her time and wait for the right moment.

"Lorraine, I'm truly sorry for the mess I made and I'm sorry you were put in this joint. I wanna make it up to ya. I just don't know what to do to make it right."

"I don't know how long I gotta stay in here, but if it's up to my ma, it'll be 'til I'm twenty-one! And they make me go to church every Sunday and the way the priest looks at us girls … Carl, I hafta pretend that I'm a good Catholic and that ain't right, is it?"

"No, it ain't. Say, I got a helluva plan to spring ya outta here. I'll agree to marry ya."

Mom's jaw dropped, "Whaaat? What if I don't agree?"

"Then you can rot in here 'til yer twenty-one, I guess," he sneered.

My mom would hold the fact over his head that she could call his probation officer at any time; any time until the statute of limitations ran out. At which time, another plot for revenge would commence.

"Okay Carl, I'll marry you, not now, but when I turn eighteen. My ma would never give permission."

"I don't know if I can wait that long," Carl huffed.

"You're gonna have to."

On October tenth, 1936, my parents were married at the Ramsey County Courthouse in Saint Paul, Minnesota. They made their home in an old three-bedroom bungalow, a block from the Mississippi River, in West Saint Paul. From the front porch of their home, they could see the homely skyline of downtown Saint Paul, with its squat, masonry buildings.

As long as their marriage lasted, they only had procreative sex. Otherwise, my mother would lay a two-by-four down the middle of their double-bed. She kept a .22 caliber revolver in her nightstand, should he violate her terms of their marriage.

The first-born of their procreative contract was my brother Kenny in 1938. Then Susan in 1941 and Ann in 1947. I came along in 1950.

Over the years, I've saved pictures of my family, keeping them in a shoebox. Among them are Mom and Dad's wedding picture. Actually, only a snapshot, turned sepia-toned with age. It could've been taken by the judge himself, or his assistant, or a witness, or his wife. Perhaps she played all three parts. My mother had grown an inch in the two years since taken from her home. She then was five-feet nothing. In the picture, she's wearing a calf-length billowy dress. The expression on her face is a mix of disgust and boredom. My dad's expression was a lot different. He stood in a borrowed, too-small sport coat, thumbs in his belt, glaring at the camera with dark, threatening eyes beneath black, scowling eyebrows. His upper lip curled in a snarl. His hair stood up in places, slicked down on the sides. He had the appearance and demeanor that Humphrey Bogart had in *Petrified Forest.*

Dad liked living in West Saint Paul. Sometimes he picked up jobs for the PWA and occasionally as a handyman. He turned into a skilled carpenter. Skilled when he wasn't drunk. Mom allowed him his ration of rotgut. I think what he liked most was that we lived within walking distance to the caverns on Wabasha Street.

Prior to the ratification of the Twenty-first Amendment, ending Prohibition, bootleggers found a hideout in the caves where they could avoid hostile Saint Paul and Ramsey County law enforcement by escaping to West Saint Paul in Dakota County. After 1933, new faces, far more vicious criminals than the cheerful bootleggers, took up residence in the caves. My dad liked to rub shoulders with these characters.

There was a family rumor that he moved up in the gangster ranks and did jobs for some of the big boys. He never dismissed the rumors including doing hits for some of them using ropes, knives, guns, or hammers. He'd sometimes come home with, what looked like smears of blood on his pants. Whenever we noticed, he would just shrug. He had two so-so paying jobs and one well-paid job which put food on the table. Mom did her part as well, by working at Woolworth's lunch counter.

In those days, better-off people would invite worse-off people into their homes for dinner. When Dad was "working," he was a free man, but when he was home, he felt that he was back at Waupun. Mom never missed a chance to humiliate him—or emasculate him—especially in front of others. For example, neighbors would be seated at the dinner table and she'd remind him that the rusty screens needed to be painted before he could eat. Afterwards, he had a cold dinner by himself, at a card table on the porch.

Because we lived so close to the river, the house had no basement and stood on two courses of cement blocks. The wooden steps to the covered front porch, were left open on its sides. All manner of wildlife could get under the house, so a good supply of rat poison was kept in the pantry. Even though the porch was roofed, it was open. The floor consisted of loose, rough planks held up by joists. A plain wooden door opened into the house. Dad spent much of his time on the porch.

Shortly after I was born, my dad bought a new radio. It was a large console type, the brand of which I don't recall, but it looked like a nice piece of furniture. I remember that when our favorite shows were on, we'd sit and watch the light behind the dial, putting our imaginations to work.

One day in March 1952, my mom flew into a rage after hearing the news report that President Truman, while giving a speech at the Jefferson-Jackson Day Dinner, said he wouldn't be seeking another term as president. "How can ... why did he do this?" Mom asked Dad.

"Well," Dad replied, "he wasn't gettin' any co-operation from Congress, especially after he fired MacArthur."

"Shut up, Carl! Take your bottle and go sit on the porch!"

Mom had other ways to punish my dad. When the Braves moved from Boston to Milwaukee, they became his favorite team. He even sent for a ballcap in the mail. When it came, he ripped open the package and slapped the cap on. After that, he was rarely seen without it. Besides, he was down to a few strands of hair on top of

120

his head. The cap was a beauty, though; blue, with red bill and a big, white M. Every chance he had, he'd listen to the games on the radio. However, if he was drunk and raucous, my mom would march across the room and snap the radio off, or spin the dial to music.

One time when she spun to music, Marty Robbins was warbling his hit crossover, forlorn, love lost, "A white sport coat (and a pink carnation)." It was a sad song and Mom dabbed her eyes with a handkerchief.

"Why the hell do ya listen to that crap? It's a stupid song!"

"What do you know about it, dumbass?" Mom stopped calling him by his name. "I never went to prom."

"You didn't stay in school," he foolishly said.

"I couldn't because of you!"

I remember this clearly, because I thought she was going to kill him. She turned and went to their bedroom, to the nightstand and opened the drawer. She thought of her children if she was sent to prison and didn't do anything except banish him to the porch, the adult equivalent of making a child sit in the corner.

Sociologists world-wide, have said there is a certain family dynamic in which one child plays the part of a mascot; another child, usually the oldest, plays the scapegoat. In my family's case, I was the mascot and my dad was the scapegoat. My older brother, Kenny, escaped being the scapegoat. He was a good-looking kid who had no broken heart issues. No Marty Robbins prom issues, either. He went to two proms with his high school sweetheart. As soon as they graduated, they were married and got the hell away from their families.

Although with Kenny gone, I was happy to have a bedroom to myself, but a new unforeseen problem arose.

I overheard my sister Susan tell my dad that if he ever sexually abused Ann, she'd kill him. I was only nine and didn't quite get it, until my dad began preying on me.

He came into my bedroom one night, smelling of cheap booze. "Billy, I'll do ya favors if ya do some favors for me."

"What kind of favors?"

121

"I'll give ya a ride ta school in my new pickup, each and every day. Beats ridin' the bus, don't it?"

"I guess so. What favor do you want me to do for you?"

He told me what to do for him and it was the most terrifying and shameful thing that ever happened to me. I was scared shitless of him. In the spring and summer, he'd reward me by taking me to Saints home games. This went on until July, when I told my mom what he was doing to me. Between sobs, I told her all the graphic details. She looked at the ceiling and blinked away tears.

Mom had often told me that she was my protector, no matter what.

She gave my sisters some money and told them to take in a movie downtown. "Billy, you're staying with me."

My dad was out on the porch reading his newspaper. Mom went to him and asked him if he wanted a cup of coffee. He was surprised at the unusual offer; unusual because she never offered before. He said, "Sure."

"Billy," she whispered, "go into the pantry and get a box of rat poison." I didn't ask why and brought it to her. I watched her put a teaspoon of the stuff, then another half-teaspoon into the coffee mug, added coffee and stirred. Without looking at me, she told me to bring it to him. I watched as he brought the cup to his lips.

"Hey, Lorraine! This smells funny! Whaddja put in this? Billy, tell your ma to pour me another cup."

"Billy," she whispered again, ya know where I keep my .22?" I nodded and went to her bedroom.

"Do ya hate him as much as I do?" I said I did and tiptoed onto the porch. It was the Fourth of July and the neighbors were already shooting off firecrackers that early afternoon. There he was, newspaper in front of him, wearing his Braves cap. My hands were shaking as I leveled the pistol at the back of his head. I fired. A cloud of acrid gunpowder rose in the humid air as my dad fell forward onto the card table. I looked around to see if any of the neighbors saw me. Luckily, they didn't and continued with their firecrackers. Mom took the gun from my shaking hands.

His head was twisted to the right and I just stood there gaping at his blood seeping from one ear and one nostril. His Braves cap had blown off. The bullet must've caught part of it. The hot, piece of lead entered, but didn't exit his skull. Fortunately, I suppose.

I snapped out of my trance when Mom said, "Now, we've got some work to do."

We removed a few of the loose boards and pushed his body down into the opening, then put the boards back in place. Mom scrubbed the card table and took it into the house. I brought the chair in. We burned Dad's cherished cap. I began hating the Braves because I hated him.

Mom was smart. She filed a missing person report with the police. After about a month, they gave up looking for him. For a few nights, I lay awake in bed and listened to the animals fight over Dad's remains. The larger animals dragged the bones away so they could gnaw on them in private.

A good citizen of West Saint Paul, told police that he found some bones down by the river. The police investigated and at first, dismissed them as animal bones until they found a shinbone, a couple of ribs and finally a skull. Human bones. But, they had no idea to whom they formerly belonged, or if it had been more than one person. Carl Wilkins was never found.

I've lived in many places over the years, but finally returned to West Saint Paul. I bought a house on a hill overlooking where our house used to be. It doesn't exist anymore. The city council decided to do what they called a "revitalization project" which actually meant bulldozing the entire neighborhood.

I still keep in contact with my siblings. Mom and her people are gone. I'm not sure of who's left on my dad's side of the family and don't really care. Maybe a few psycho cousins. My mom would never allow us to see them, or even ask about them.

I live alone in a three-bedroom house, similar to the house in which I grew up. I'm twice divorced, no kids. Neither of the marriages lasted very long. I think it was because they couldn't deal with the PTSD given to me when I was nine. I can't think of any other reason.

The animal noises also remain in my memory, but they're slowly getting weaker with time and Jack Daniel's.

The escape

After all these years, I still remember the first time we met. It must've been in the spring of 2025 because I'd just finished high school. I was eighteen, scared, on the run and all alone. I smashed my cell phone against a tree, realizing that it could be used to track me. Escaping from Des Moines, taking the backroads, I bicycled about twenty miles per day. After five days, exhausted, I stopped about ten miles short of Audubon and looked around for an overnight shelter. Five days on the road without bathing, meant that I smelled so bad, I wouldn't want to be downwind of myself.

Did I have a plan? No. The only thing I had to do, if I valued my health, was to avoid larger cities.

While walking with my bike, I saw him. He was sitting in a lawn chair reading a book. I walked a few feet closer. He shaded his eyes.

"Who are you? What are you doing here?"

I walked closer so that he would be in my shadow. He looked like somebody who at the time, I thought was old; maybe forty-five, or even fifty, though he had a full head of dark hair. I told him that I'd come from Des Moines and that my name was Sally Treville.

"Yeah, my parents had a sense of humor. They named me after Sally Hemmings."

"Thomas Jefferson's mistress."

"Exactly."

"My name is Bob Simmons." We shook hands. "Your last name's Treville. Is that French?"

"I guess. About a hundred years ago, it was Demontreville, but we dropped the *demon* part of it."

"That was a wise choice." I couldn't help laughing when he said this. I liked him from that moment on.

"I've only got one lawn chair, but you can have it. You look tired."

I asked Bob what he did for a living. He said he used to be an American History professor at Grinnell.

"Used to be? What happened at Grinnell?" I asked.

"They fired me for teaching the truth. I refused to help them re-write history to suit their ideologies."

"Was it that Christian American Citizens' League?"

"Yes, they've infiltrated every level of government and most institutions. I'm sure they didn't realize that the acronym would be CACL. I think it's apropos, don't you?"

"Cackle isn't spelled that way," I said.

"Close enough. You're traveling alone? So, where's your family?"

"They were murdered." I tried not to, but I choked on the words. "My mom and dad and my little sister and brother were shot to death in our house. I wasn't home."

"What? Shot to death? Do they know who did it?"

"I'm sure they do, but they're not going to do anything about it." Now, I couldn't stop the sobs and the tears. "We were a happy family. Mom and Dad had good jobs and made good money. So, we could afford to have nice things. Some people hated us for being successful and didn't want us to live a good life."

"That sounds like the work of the Citizens' League."

"It seems that they can't be stopped. How could we let this happen?"

"How did Nazi Germany happen? Sally, it's almost the same thing. Some people don't really know the people for whom they're voting. They're blind to the issues! And look around you, this is the result."

"When did it start, Bob?"

"I think it began before you were born. Starting small and benign, then building momentum. Some of us knew that mixing conservative politics with religious fundamentalism wouldn't work out so well. But, when they took over the military, any battle *we* wage would be a losing one."

"So, we're both running away, Bob?"

"That would be correct, I'm afraid."

We started driving toward Audubon. I left my bike behind. No great loss.

Poor Bob, I stank so badly that when I got into his car, he rolled down all the windows.

There wasn't much of anything in Audubon, except a little Mom and Pop restaurant and a bar. I washed up in the restaurant bathroom, changed clothes, thought about burning the dirty ones and tried to tame my hair.

We were devising a plan regarding what we were going to do next. I was glad to be part of the *We*, except that I didn't know how long I was to be part of the plan.

Bob plugged in his car to charge it and said that it would be enough to get us to Minnesota.

"Minnesota? Why Minnesota?" I asked.

"Because," he said, "Minnesota isn't likely to become radicalized. The National Guard, Highway Patrol and local police are loyal to their governor. They also have help from volunteer militias."

"What about other states?"

"I feel that California, New York and Massachusetts will make a stand, as well."

"Okay," I said, "we're going to Minnesota, then what?"

"I'll cross the border into Minnesota and move on into Canada. I might be able to get a teaching job up there."

"I want to ask you something. Can I come with you? I've got a passport."

We ate some food, the car was charged and our next stop in Iowa was Rock Rapids, due north on Highway 75.

"I hope we don't run into a problem traveling together. You know, my being a young woman and bi-racial."

"That's why we're taking less-traveled roads. Besides, if we draw anyone's attention, I'm just a dad on a road trip with his daughter."

"But, I don't even look anything like you."

"Okay, which one of your parents was black?"

"My dad was black and my mom was white."

"Well, Sally, just turn that around. I'm your white dad and your mom is black."

I wanted to put up an argument about the matter, but it was too logical to disagree.

We made it to Rock Rapids without the incident that I had imagined. It was only another small, decaying, rural town. We never drove at night and always hit the road at dawn. Our next destination was Ash Creek, Minnesota.

At Ash Creek, we were met by state troopers, about seven of them and they were wearing combat gear. Two approached the car, one on each side.

"Driver's license and registration," one of them said to Bob, "where ya headed?"

"Canada," Bob answered.

He wanted to see our passports, as well. Then, a man identifying himself as Major something or other came over and examined our passports himself.

"Who's the girl?" he asked, looking at me.

"She's my daughter," Bob said.

"Well," said the Major, "how come she's got a different last name?"

"She decided to use her mother's maiden name."

Bob managed to keep a straight face while I bit the inside of my cheeks to keep from laughing.

That statement flew over the Major's head.

"You carrying any firearms?" Bob was asked.

"Yes, a 9-mm handgun and a 12-gauge. They're in the trunk and the ammo's in the glove box."

"At least you came prepared. You better take them out of the trunk and keep them where you can reach them. 'Cause you never know what might happen."

Bob agreed, but asked, "Isn't that against the law?"

"It was, but things are different now."

The Major called a man over and told him to remove the license plates and tape a fake permit to the back window. Iowa plates wouldn't be too popular in Minnesota.

We also learned that Minnesota had shut down her borders. No one in and no one out, except for those traveling to Canada. We were directed to stay on Highway 75 to East 90 to North 35. The Major told us that the main highways were patrolled more frequently.

Driving across the width and length of Minnesota, we shared driving duties. After all, I had a learner's permit and he was my white dad.

Bob had told me that he withdrew all of his money from the bank. He never told me how much it was and I never asked. He just seemed to be spending a lot of money on food and lodging. And paying for separate rooms.

I enjoyed his company and often found myself staring at him as he drove. He wasn't exactly unattractive. In fact, I thought he was getting better looking every day. Then, I had a thought. What would it be like to go to bed with an older, white guy? How much different would it be from having sex with a skinny teenager? Bob was certainly easier to talk to.

We talked about everything, especially history and politics.

"Bob, why didn't the president say anything against the Christian Americans Citizens' League? He just lets them do anything they want because they're in the majority in Congress."

"Don't be naïve, Sally. He's one of them. And don't forget there are five of them on the Supreme Court. This country may never be the same. It might take a revolution or another civil war to make things right again. Realistically, though, our side would lose badly."

Highway 35 took us to Duluth, where we saw the Coast Guard patrolling the waters of Lake Superior. We were surprised when we learned that they were on our side. Bob said that he wasn't sure that the FBI, the CIA and the NSA would be on our side and assumed that they would want to be on the winning side, in the event of war.

Past Duluth, we went across Grand Portage State Park where we crossed the Pigeon River into Ontario, Canada. Our passports were scanned and we were waved through. No questions asked. We continued on to Thunder Bay.

We stayed at the Prince Edward Hotel, where I talked Bob into getting a single room. He didn't balk at the idea and it made me wonder if he felt the same way about me that I felt about him.

We had sex and I found that his technique was adequate and with a little more practice, it might get better. Of course, he said it was great. But, we practiced and practiced 'til we got it right.

After a particularly fantastic session and when I was alone, I'd whisper, "Sally Simmons." That sounded much too sibilant and decided that I'd stick to Treville with no damn hyphen.

Bob and I went opposite ways. He to the University of Vancouver, B.C., to teach World History and I went to the University of Ottawa to learn World History. We enjoyed our passionate goodbyes and promised to stay in touch. We broke that promise right after we left each other.

A couple of years later, I was horrified to learn that the U.S. military defeated the rebel forces in less than a month. Yes, it was inevitable, but still, the America I once knew, was no more. Hundreds of thousands of "enemies of the state" all across the country, were crowded into internment camps for re-education.

After earning my Bachelor's degree, I married a professor at the University of Ottawa, a white guy. I've come to like vanilla. Thanks, Bob.

I finished school with a Master's in education and Marc, my husband, got me into the history department.

I didn't change my last name and Marc said that he didn't mind.

Occasionally, I still think about Bob Simmons and hope that he's alive and doing well. I'm thinking that maybe next summer, I'll take a trip to Vancouver and find out. Marc may want to tag along.

R eading the obituaries, I saw that Jackson Ellsworth had died. I already knew that, because I wrote the notice myself. I had to do it because *Variety* couldn't find his file. The truth is, they never prepared one. I made certain the obituary was titled: "Silent Film Star Dies." In my estimation, he was a star even though he was always a member of the supporting cast. After a short career on the New York stage, of which he was often a leading man, he was the second lead in twenty-eight silent feature films between 1912 to 1930.

His funeral would not draw the thousands of adoring, grieving fans as did Rudolph Valentino's. The only thing that Ellsworth and Valentino had in common was that they both were interred at Forest Lawn.

W hen Ellsworth's agent, Max Avery retired, I was asked to take Max's place to make sure that our agency retain Ellsworth as a client. At first, I couldn't imagine why we'd want to keep him, but it made it appear as though we had a client who was ready and willing to take on any roles which were offered. One lucrative role was about to be offered to him.

After picking up parts in local theater, Jackson lived in reclusion for the past decade. I phoned him in the summer of 1954 and said, without elaborating, that I had an offer for a continuing role on television. He sounded enthusiastic and told me to come right over. I, however, was less than enthusiastic because he habitually turned down scripts. I couldn't blame him for recently turning down an off-screen, prologue narration for a cheesy, science fiction movie.

Driving through the Hollywood Hills, nestled among the mansions, I found a simple, squat bungalow and felt that I had to verify the address. There were two large arborvitaes flanking the door and rose bushes, one yellow, the other pink, near each corner of the house.

A dark and handsome, young Latino man opened the door.

"I'm Jim Harrison."

"Oh yes, Mr. Ellsworth is expecting you. Won't you come in?" He smiled and gestured with a sweep of his arm and led me to a dining room and again, held out his arm.

"Please sit down, Mr. Ellsworth will be here, momentarily."

I don't know why I was surprised, but his diction was perfect with only a whisper of an accent. Looking around the room at the floor-to-ceiling bookcase covering an entire wall, I imagined that the room doubled as a library or den. In the corner stood a television console cabinet with its doors closed, as if to conceal what it was.

I stood when Jackson Ellsworth entered the room.

"Mr. Ellsworth?"

"Call me Jackson and I'll call you Jim."

We shook hands. I felt shabbily dressed in my sport coat, no necktie and baggy khakis, while he wore a navy-blue pinstriped, expertly tailored suit with a lighter blue ascot.

"Let's sit down."

I was mildly amazed that his hair had only thinned a little and had turned a silver-gray as did his pencil-thin mustache which contrasted with his deep tan. He had aged extremely well for a man in his mid-sixties. He was tall, about six-one, still good looking and his physique was as slim as it had always been.

"I see you met my houseboy, Carlos. I don't think I could ever do without him. He's so much help to me. He chauffeurs me around, takes me wherever I want to go, runs errands … tell me about this terrific part …" he interrupted himself. "Television, you say?"

"Yes, it's a recurring role as host of a weekly drama series. Everything's on film and you would introduce each show. They may have you do the lead-ins for commercials. I always want you to know that I pushed quite hard on your behalf. At first, they were reluctant, because you haven't appeared before a camera in over twenty years, but said that they may grant you an audition."

"I don't know, Jim. I mean, I like television. I have one in here and Carlos has one in his bedroom. While I prefer Milton Berle,

Carlos likes Ed Sullivan. He gets a big kick out of watching tutu-wearing, dancing bears. I digress. Where were we? What's the show called and how much does it pay? I'm not going to take it unless they pay well. Will I have any lines?"

"Five thousand a week, guaranteed, for twenty-six weeks with an option for an additional twenty-six and your lines are on cue cards. All you have to do, is sit in a wing-back chair and read the cards. I don't know if they have a title for it yet, but these shows are usually named for the sponsor."

"I'll do it! When can I start? Where do I sign?"

"Some of the dramas have already been filmed, so they're just waiting for the network to give them a start date and a time slot. My guess is that it would begin next month, around Labor Day. When I receive more information, I'll call you. Then I'll set up an audition date for you."

"Do you know what else I like about television? All the live plays … it's a perfect medium for them. But, those soap operas are dreadful! Carlos, bring tall, iced teas for Mr. Harrison and myself, or do you prefer something stronger, Jim?"

"No, iced tea would be fine."

Carlos came into the room and placed the glasses on coasters. Each glass contained three, stacked ice cubes. Carlos poured the tea from a pitcher.

"You're probably wondering how I came to live in such a small house. It was due mainly to income tax, together with the crash of '29. I had to sell my large home and purchase this one. It's still rather nice, don't you think?"

"Yes, it looks comfortable."

"You know that when I first came out here, I wanted to be in westerns. They had asked me if I knew how to ride a horse. I think they were hoping that I couldn't. I landed a part after explaining that I had been riding since I was seven. I mean, just because I was from upstate New York … would you care for a cigar? They're Cuban. *Cohibas.*"

I accepted and watched him clip the ends of both thin, dark cigars. We continued to talk about silent films, the forgotten stars and the studios. I had to get back to the office and said my goodbyes. He seemed to enjoy our conversation and I attributed that to his and Carlos' lack of visitors. Both of them waved from the doorway as I drove away.

About three weeks later, I received a phone call from Carlos. Between anguished sobs, he told me that he'd gone shopping for Mr. Ellsworth and when he returned, he found Jackson lying on the floor, dead.

"What? How?" I shouted.

"One of the ambulance men said that he thought it looked like a heart attack."

I offered my condolences and told him that I would attend the funeral. I called the studio and told them what happened. They said it was okay and decided to go with their second choice. Randolph Scott was their first choice, but he turned up his nose at television.

In a twisted way, I'm glad that Jackson was dead because I wouldn't have had the heart to tell him that he lost the part to Ronald Reagan.

n the whole, my childhood was unremarkable, but pleasant enough, except for a few rough spots. One of which occurred when I was in second grade.

There was a bully in my class who went by the name of P.J. He didn't look like anyone would expect a bully to look like. P.J. was a midget who stood about two-feet ten. He was also best friends with Everett Barnes, a much larger bully. Since P.J. was the "brains of the outfit," I guess that made Everett the "toady."

Everett would perform the daily ritual of lifting P.J. up to the classroom pencil sharpener so that P.J. could sharpen his half-dozen pencils into deadly, needle tips. Then, he'd run around the classroom and stab as many kids as he could, before the teacher walked in. Everett was his bodyguard, so no one dared to say anything against P.J. or, god forbid, do anything to that junior psycho.

I still bear one of the graphite scars on my back, where he nailed me. To this day, I hate the little prick!

Probably what gripes me the most, is that adults always believed his innocence because after doing something destructive, he had what could best be described as a "what, who me?" look on his stupid, little, criminal face.

One day while in school, I watched him tumble down a flight of slate steps. He lay at the bottom, crumpled, screaming and sobbing. It was a good thing for me, that Everett wasn't around, or P.J. might've told Everett that I had pushed him.

Other children heard his cries and gathered around the stairwell. It was, what could be called, a moment of single-minded solidarity. So, at long last, after waiting for almost an entire school year, revenge was ours! Soon, we all were laughing and clapping with delight.

I've always wondered what P.J. is doing these days, nearly fifty years later. Would he still be alive, or was he murdered by somebody? I was thinking about him the other day, while watching the news and apparently, the lead story was about a midget who boarded an airliner with a fistful of sharp pencils and began stabbing passengers and flight attendants.

The TV reporter went on to say that the pilot stormed out of the cockpit and threw the midget against the bulkhead, rendering him unconscious. The reporter added that the midget's motive and identity were unknown.

"Get him," I screamed, "it's P.J.!"

ow remember," my court-appointed attorney advised, "forget about Descartes and his theories and just concentrate on what you need to say, to get your release from the hospital. The judge is going to ask you simple, but specific questions about historical facts."

Okay, I thought to myself, going over a litany of possible questions and answers. *The U.S.* lost *World War Two, won in a war with Korea and never had a war with Viet Nam.* Of course, I knew differently, but I didn't want to go back to the State Hospital.

A few months before, I had been trying to explain to my wife and daughter that certain things and events, both current and past, didn't seem right. It was as if there was a pattern unfolding, but it was the wrong one ... the wrong continuum. Somehow, time and history had taken an alternate route and it changed the present course of events and it would also change the future. That's when my wife signed my commitment papers. She told me it was for my own good.

I had to forget everything I had known about the *real* past and tell everyone that it was only a dream. My attorney told me that I had to help work on my own defense. I listened to all the news on the radio, read newspapers every day and read all the American and World History books that I could find at the library.

I was amused, but not surprised, to find the United States, with its ally, Mexico, was at war with Texas. Following the Civil War, Texas had decided to secede from the Confederacy to become a separate country and refused to join the Union. They had most of the oil and refineries. Surrounded on all sides and getting severely thrashed, we only had to wait for their surrender. That war was in its eighth year. We were also simultaneously engaged in a protracted war with Denmark and Sweden. We had no allies with the exception of Mexico. Former allies France, Italy, Israel and Portugal declined our invitation to help us. We had also elected, by an overwhelming majority, the shortest president, at four-feet six, with an intellect to match. I found it no less preposterous than the election of his predecessor, an out of work standup comedian.

Finally, my court date had arrived and my case was presented to the judge. I admitted that I wrongfully perceived reality because of a recurring nightmare. My attorney congratulated me when the judge declared me sane and ordered my release from the hospital.

To celebrate, my wife suggested that we take a trip to Peterson, D.C. "Besides enjoying the trip ourselves," she remarked, "it will be educational for our daughter."

We drove to downtown Kansas City and boarded the jet train. Reaching the outskirts of Portland, we took a dirigible to the Capitol. For the three weeks we were there, we stayed at the Arlington Resort.

We took a lot of pictures and had a wonderful time looking at them when we got home. Of particular interest, were the ones we took at the Jones Memorial. Every school kid knows he was our ninth president who had become a hero in our Great War with Switzerland. He had served only one year when, during his State of the Union address, he was attacked and slain by his vice president, with a ball peen hammer. Vice President Presley was hanged moments later, in the Capitol rotunda.

"Look Papa-san," exclaimed Misako, "President Jones is lying inside his Memorial, just as he is on the three-dollar bill!"

"Why yes, yes he is," I replied.

oad closed

I t's been said that story telling is a lost art. Sure, there are novelists and short story writers, but can they verbalize their stories as the ancients had done? Those pre-book people sat around the camp-fire and usually, the eldest member of the group would spin an oral history relating to his or her family. The original story probably got embellished each time it was told. A little hyperbolizing to make it more interesting. Most great storytellers are part actors, part sales-people, but mostly, highly-accomplished bullshitters.

It was on the occasion of my sixty-sixth birthday and retirement party. My small family had gathered at my home to celebrate; two grown daughters, their kids, one son-in-law and, of course, my wife. My oldest daughter left her lazy husband after two years. I wasn't even done paying for her wedding!

Yes, I was presented with a cake from the bakery. I had previously begged my wife not to put those stupid little candles on it. I hated blowing them out. I watched other people blow out their candles and sometimes, whenever I saw spit flying, I'd suddenly lose my appetite for cake. And I hated when wax got onto the frosting. I like cake, sans candles, with butter crème frosting and large rosettes. It was my birthday and I insisted on getting a large wedge with a rosette.

After we demolished the cake and drank enough coffee, I wanted to tell my grandchildren the story I've told many times to my wife and daughters. The four of them, including the son-in-law, retreated to the kitchen to make another pot of coffee. Although they'd heard the story before, they listened for any improvised changes to the story line. I'd never change the ending.

My granddaughter, Lisa, my favorite, and oldest of my grandkids, is my oldest daughter's kid. She had graduated high school already. What am I saying? She's a sophomore at the university. Time seems to accelerate after fifty. Lisa sat the closest to me. The two boys, my youngest daughter's kids, sat on the couch. Bobby, in ninth grade and his brother, Dave, who I think is in seventh grade, both came over without their I-pods, for which I was grateful. It won't be too much longer that I'll be able to call Bobby, Bobby. I'm sure he'll want to be called, Rob, or Bob.

"It's story time," I announced, "and it's all true! So, listen up and listen tight," I said doing a passable, I thought, impression of John Wayne. The reference was lost on my audience.

"It all began over twenty years ago. I was about as old as your mother is now, Lisa."

"Wow!" interjected Dave, "you were old, even twenty years ago!"

"Shut up, Dave! I wanna hear this," scolded Bobby.

"Anyway," I continued, "your grandma and I had an argument one night and I couldn't sleep and while she dozed off, I took a drive across town to cool off. I turned onto a short street and came to a stop, close to two sawhorse barricades, painted in luminous orange with the words, 'Road Closed' written on them. There were railroad tracks glinting in the moonlight and identical barricades on the opposite side of the tracks. Then, I heard a train and saw the headlight. It was an Amtrak passenger train with only two cars being pulled. I noted that it was 11:07 p.m. In the first car, I saw passengers looking at me and I waved to them. Some waved back. The passengers in the second car, however, appeared to be more boisterous. They waved with more enthusiasm. Many of them were pressing their hands to the windows. Others were hitting the windows with their fists. And they looked like they were yelling something. The train's horn bleated a long blast, followed by a bell, then it picked up speed and was gone.

"The next night, about the same time, I returned to the railroad tracks and waited. The scene was repeated, only with different people on board. When your grandma heard about what I was doing, she said I was becoming obsessed with the whole thing. I disregarded her criticism and drove to the tracks a third time. Again, the train flew by and again, the peoples' behavior in the second car was the same. Only I thought their actions did seem to be more panicky than boisterous. Perhaps it was just my imagination. On those three nights, the train was crossing that street between 11:05 and 11:18 p.m.

"Despite of grandma's objections, the following night, I went driving a little bit earlier and stopped at the Amtrak depot to ask questions about that train. The man behind the counter, stared blankly at me and said, 'You musta been seein' things, mister. Amtrak only runs two trains arriving and departing to and from the northwest and not at those times.' He pulled out a schedule and showed me. 'See? This train arrives at around 2 a.m. and this train departs at 8:14 a.m. and besides, we always carry more than two cars and no, I don't know why the road is closed.' I was satisfied with his explanation, but not at all satisfied with what I'd witnessed on the previous nights.

"At 11:00 p.m., I waited by the tracks. Only this time, I got out of my car and stood near the tracks. I saw the headlight and heard the horn. The engineer must've seen me, because I could hear the brakes screeching against the rails. It came to a stop about twenty yards past me. A rather corpulent man bounded off the train with a flashlight in his hand. 'What the hell do you think you're doing?' he yelled, 'get over here!' I reluctantly walked over. He was wearing a green-striped, long-sleeved shirt and on his head, one of those high-crowned, felt hats peculiar to his and the firefighter profession. On the front of the hat was a brass plate which read, Conductor. His face was florid with anger.

"'Are ya gonna get on this time?' he demanded an answer.

"I shrugged and said that I didn't have a ticket and asked where we were supposed to be going.

"'Don't have a ticket,' he whined mockingly, 'where are we going? I've only heard that ten-thousand times!' He shone the flashlight on the steps and gestured for me to get on board. I hesitated and he bellowed, 'Get on board! We don't have all night!'

"The conductor followed me into the first car. I counted the people in the car: thirteen. There was an old woman sitting in the front row with a walker folded up, which was leaning on the empty seat next to her. She stared at me briefly, took a long drag off a cigarette and gazed out the window.

"On each side of the aisle, there were rows of three, blue, polyester seats. Most were sitting by themselves, except for a gaggle of teenagers and an elderly couple. The teenagers, seven of them, were sitting toward the back of the car, on both sides of the aisle.

They were wearing formal dress, as if they were coming from a high school prom. Four boys and three girls. One boy appeared to be holding court, while the rest of them were laughing. He glanced at me, turned back to his group, said something and they all laughed. Were they laughing at me? I didn't think they were, but I checked my fly, anyway.

"The elderly couple nodded and smiled weakly at me. Across from them, was a thin woman in her early thirties, I guessed. Her straight, ash-blond hair touched the tops of her shoulders. She wasn't wearing any makeup except for a deep shade of red lipstick which was all the more obvious on her pallid face. She held a paperback book on her lap and was wearing black-rimmed, half-frame reading glasses perched on the end of her nose. I thought she was going to look up at me, but didn't take her eyes off of the book. She crossed her legs and pulled the hem of her black skirt past her knee and checked the top button of her shiny, purple blouse.

"I headed down a few rows; there was a guy dressed in layers of clothing including a topcoat, napping. It was too warm to be dressed like that. Then I realized that he might be homeless. He wore an old, worn, tan, felt fedora with greasy stains on the brim and on the crown. There were finger-sized holes in the creases. Besides a couple of weeks of beard growth, the most disturbing thing about him was his jaundiced complexion. Kidney or liver damage, I thought. The guy wasn't that old either. He lifted the side of his hat brim to look at me with one brownish, yellowish eye, where the whites should've been.

"Sitting a few rows behind the teenagers was a black man, about my age. I sat across the aisle from him.

"'Hey, how's it goin?' he smiled at me.

"'I don't know,' I said. 'Do you know what we're doing on this train? And where the hell are we going?'

"'I don't know any more than you do, man. I got off work and went to the station to catch my commuter and that conductor,' he pointed at the conductor, who was seated at the front, facing us, 'told me I should get on this train.'

"'Where did you get on?'

"'Chicago and I don't know where we're goin' from here. I been on this train for eight hours, or it could be eight weeks, or even eight years. I just don't know. All's I know is when I got on, the old people and that homeless guy were already here. Then, the others got on and then, you.'

"'Well, maybe when it's daylight in a few hours, we can see where we're going.'

"'Listen, before I got on this train, it *was* daylight, sun shinin', but as soon as I walked in, nothin' but black as pitch out there. Did you feel that? I think we're slowin' down.'

"'Yeah, I think we are.'

"'Seems like we're gonna pick up that guy.'

"I got up and crossed the aisle to look out the window. There was a man standing under the lugubriously, amber glow of a mercury-vapor street light. The train stopped and he walked toward the train. The conductor met and led him into our car. He was well-dressed in a light gray suit, white shirt and silver-colored necktie. The light color of his clothes contrasted sharply with his deep, tan complexion and his jet-black hair was slicked back, tight against his head in a short ponytail. He was tall and thin … an in-shape kind of thin. He held a black briefcase in front of him with both hands on the handle.

"As he scanned the passengers, I couldn't help noticing his deep-set, penetrating eyes with black irises. Everyone in the car stared at him and his every movement.

"'It's time,' he said to the conductor and the portly conductor led him to the back of the car and the door to the next car. The conductor produced a ring of brass keys and unlocked the second car. It was then, that we heard the crying and screaming of those passengers. People were saying the *Lord's Prayer*, praying the Rosary, calling up whatever deity they worshipped, the Virgin Mary, God, Vishnu, Buddha. Whichever they we're hoping would help them, was apparently to no avail. The second car was uncoupled and coasted down a slight decline to a siding.

"It was then that I noticed the conductor had forgotten to re-lock the door at the end of the car, when he ushered the mysterious stranger back in. The thin man stopped and touched the shoulder of the pale, blond woman. She tossed the paperback she was reading onto the empty seat beside her. When she rose from her seat, the stranger placed his briefcase there and the three of them engaged in a whispering conference at the front of our car. She was one of them! When no one was looking, I dashed toward the front of the car, snatched the briefcase and headed for the back door. The train started to move and I leapt, landing awkwardly on one of the ties and nearly tumbled, but regained my balance and ran.

"I remember when I was younger, I ran the hundred-yard dash in ten-flat and that was when no one was chasing me and I wasn't running for my life. I heard their footfalls and angry shouts as they ran after me and I ran 'til I thought my heart would burst and my lungs would collapse. I ran 'til I could no longer hear them. It was when I felt I was safe, that I knelt down and opened the briefcase."

"What was in the briefcase, Grandpa?" all my grandchildren chimed in, even Lisa.

"It was full of shit," I replied, "just like this story."

he secret

utside the hospital window, the sun made a lazy arc across the southern sky. My dad lay with oxygen tubes up his nose, a morphine drip stuck in his arm, drifting in and out of consciousness. While I waited for his fleeting moments of lucidity, I stared out the window and fingered the copy of his Living Will, specifying DNI/DNR, which I kept in my jacket pocket. Knowing that I was there, I suppose, gave him some comfort. Both of us, however, were well-aware that the cancer, which began in his lungs, had metastasized to his other organs. He was being cannibalized from the inside out. And the smell; the stink of rot and death hovered over him. His parchment-like, jaundiced skin hung loosely from his bones. Due to several sessions of chemotherapy, he lost all of his hair, not that he had much of it left, in the first place. I self-consciously ran my fingers through my own thinning hair.

He's an old man, I told myself, but going out this way …

I had to meet with the real estate agent later that afternoon at my dad's house. It used to be my parents' house and my boyhood home. I'd been back many times in the past forty years and each time, I performed the ritual of examining every room, every fixture, every artifact. This time, I'd have to be responsible to strip it of all its furnishings … nothing left. It would be up to someone else to re-create the house in their own image.

I walked into the house and threw my jacket over an arm of the sofa. I had about fifteen minutes to look around before the real estate guy showed up. Precisely at four o'clock, the doorbell rang. He filled the doorway, short, corpulent and young. Maybe late-twenties.

"Mr. Lombardi? I'm Nelson. We spoke on the phone."

"Yes, come in." *I didn't know if Nelson was his first or last name and didn't care.*

"You wouldn't be related to Vince Lombardi, would you? He was an idol of mine. Remember, he said, 'Winning isn't everything, it's the only thing.'"

"Yes, I remember and no, we weren't related, Mr. Nelson."

"You can call me, John. Everything is all about winning. Don't you think?"

"Take off your coat. Let's sit at the dining room table and show what you've come up with."

"Well, it was hard to find comparisons; a Cape Cod of this size, five bedrooms, upper-bracket, in the winter, in this market, on a seven-acre parcel … out in the middle of … I mean secluded … tough sell. I'm afraid that I'm going to insist on a one-hundred eighty-day listing. That is, if you want your price. After all, we'd be looking for a special buyer. Will you be staying here, some of the time?"

He spread out stats and pictures on the oval table.

"I have to work in La Crosse during the week. Sundays and Mondays are my days off, so I can stay here on those days."

"What do you do in La Crosse?"

"Sell furniture."

"How's business?"

"A little slow with the high-end stuff. Could we get down to the business at hand?"

"Of course. Let's see, your home, excuse me, your father's home, was built in 1946 … boy, the economy was great back then. You could get a lot more bang for your buck … I figure it's worth about $450,000, minus some expenses and my six percent commission. I work on commission, just like you.

Just like me? You're full of shit, young man! "How about $550,000, a six percent and a one-hundred forty-day listing?"

"I don't know sir," he said, rubbing his chin, perhaps in a practiced gesture, "I guess we could try it."

"And let's not call it a five-bedroom. Call it a three, with den and office."

"Fine. We'll be looking at all offers." He took a large, electronic lockbox from his briefcase. "Can I put this on the front door?"

"No, put it on the railing."

"Okay. If you want to sign the listing and commission contract, while I measure the rooms."

"I'll wait 'til you're done, if you don't mind."

John Nelson, Realtor extraordinaire, probably thought that my dad was a little strange for having acoustic tiles on the ceiling and walls of his office, even on the inside of the door and deep-pile carpeting on the floor. The reason was for soundproofing. A long ago disconnected phone, a secure line, still sat on the corner of Dad's cherry wood desk.

Jouncing down the stairs, Nelson asked, "So what does, did your father do?"

"Insurance agent," I answered while examining the papers in front of me.

"I'm guessing that you have power of attorney."

"Yes."

"Okay, sign your name and below it, write 'for Alan Lombardi."

He gathered up the papers and headed for the door.

"Now, go out there and win one for the Gipper," I told him.

Nelson turned back and asked, "What? Who's that?"

"Never mind." I waved goodbye and thought that my reference to the Gipper, whether it referred to Ronnie Reagan or George Gip, evidently eluded him.

I watched him drive away in his dark, blue Ford, down the long, gravel driveway, turning left onto the main road.

Until I was about twelve, I believed that my dad was an insurance agent with Mutual of Omaha. He'd leave, sometimes for days or weeks at a time, saying that he had to go to the main office. My mom would say her goodbyes, smile and tell him, "Good luck on your presentation."

I'd assumed that he was driving to Omaha, which was to the west, but each time, he turned east toward Madison. I never questioned either of my parents, but whenever I heard them talking in hushed tones, I thought something was up. Something secretive.

The three of us had separate bedrooms. My mom, a victim of childhood rheumatic fever, had taken to her bed after her first heart attack. At the age of thirty-two, she suffered her second heart attack and died. My dad, two years older than she, suddenly found himself a widower and a single parent. It was from that moment, that he seemed to age quickly.

I was born in 1949 to a stay-at-home mom and a successful salesman. We never seemed to have a lack of money and in retrospect, I suppose they spoiled me, being their only child. I didn't notice it at the time.

My parents were two attractive people. My dad was slim and tall with dark, straight hair slicked back and often had a pipe clenched between his teeth. I can still remember the fragrant aroma of the tobacco. My mom was a little shorter, also slim with long, curly, copper-colored hair. They dressed fashionably and always, even at home, were well-mannered and maintained an air of civility.

When I turned nineteen, my dad advised me to go to college and try to achieve and keep a high grade-point average. "You know," he'd say, "to keep from getting drafted."

Since the war in Viet Nam was still raging, I took his advice and enrolled at the University of Wisconsin-Milwaukee. He had been in World War Two as an intelligence officer and was sent to the European Theater. He never saw combat, but was concerned that, as a draftee, I would.

During spring break, my freshman year, I came home. He sat me down at the kitchen table and said, "There's something I've been meaning to tell you." He packed his pipe with his thumb. I offered him my lighter, but he waved it off and had a kitchen match ready.

"What is it, Dad?" I waited while he took two long puffs.

"I never left home on insurance business. Oh, I might've sold a couple of policies a year, only to keep up appearances. After the war, they were looking for college educated people with some experience in the intelligence field."

"Who's they?" I interrupted.

He sat back in his chair, took another puff, then leaned forward, "The CIA, the Agency, the Company."

I laughed and he looked at me quizzically. "I've known it for years."

"But, how?"

"Your locked soundproofed office, the secure phone, the long-distance calls to and from Virginia, the visitors at all hours. It all added up. I thought that either you were in the Cosa Nostra or the CIA, or something like that. Mom covered up for you too, didn't she?"

"She did to protect you, and herself of course.

"Don't say no now, but after you graduate, I could put in a good word for you at the Agency."

"I don't know. I mean I'd like to live a normal life, not skulking around and acting paranoid all the time."

"Hey, *I* wasn't paranoid. I might've caused paranoia, through."

"Well, what did you do? Tell me about some of your missions?"

"We called them, assignments. I'll tell you one. A very important one. It was in 1957, September, when Eisenhower signed the first Civil Rights Act into law. We uncovered a piece of intelligence that someone in the Klan was going to assassinate him."

"So, what was your involvement? How was it prevented?"

"Those dipshit rednecks blamed Ike for passing the law, so they were going to send their best squirrel hunter to open fire on his motorcade on its way to Camp David. The Klan had their own intelligence apparatus: the newspapers. Whenever Ike did anything, anything at all, it made the papers."

"Did the CIA send you to prevent it? What about the FBI or the Secret Service?"

"The FBI," he grinned, "was still busy red-baiting, even though Joe McCarthy was dead and buried and the Secret Service wanted to simply cancel Ike's trip and keep him under wraps 'til the thing blew over. The Agency, on the other hand, wanted to draw the potential assassin out and immobilize him."

"You mean to kill him?"

"Yes, of course. The chosen assassin was also a Georgia State Trooper and it was fairly easy to track him. He drove his own car up to D.C. I was given a few photos of him, including one wearing his trooper's uniform. I guess he wanted to do it for God, country and governor."

"Did you have anything to do with killing him?"

"I had everything to do with it."

"My God! How many others did you kill?"

"He was the only one. We accessed his phone records and found that he had made a hotel reservation in Washington. A real flea trap! I waited for him in that stinking lobby for only about ten minutes. Then he appeared, a large man, wearing a straw cowboy hat and a cheap looking black suit. He was headed straight for the door, not walking particularly fast. I carried a Washington Post in front of me and bumped into him. I had a long-needled syringe, filled with cyanide, behind it. I said, 'Excuse me,' and watched him swagger out the door. I followed and saw his swagger turn into a stagger. It looked like he had a sudden heart attack. He never made it to his car which, it was discovered, had a rifle in the backseat with a blanket over it."

"I only heard about what the CIA was doing … killing certain people in this country and other countries, but …"

"C'mon son, don't be so naïve! Sometimes we had to get our hands dirty to ensure our own country's freedom and way of life."

"When did you start with the CIA?"

"In 1948, just before you were born and quit shortly after the trooper assignment. Nine years was enough."

"Dad, be honest. Did the CIA … did they have anything at all to do with the Kennedy assassination?"

"I don't know … hardly anyone knows for sure. It's still being debated. But, I will tell you this: JFK was highly critical of our operations and was quoted as saying that he wanted to 'shred the CIA into a thousand pieces and scatter them to the four winds.' So, maybe you can come up with your own answer."

After I graduated from the University with a B.A. I got married and moved to La Crosse. Two years later, she took off for Reno and filed for divorce. I went back home to see my dad and pour my heart out. I needed sympathy.

He listened for a while and asked why she was divorcing me. I told him that we were incompatible.

My dad never had much room for humor in his life and never told a joke, so there I sat in stunned astonishment when he said,

"Incompatible? You have no income and she isn't pat-able? …
Henny Youngman." He laughed, while I scowled. He pounded out
the ashes of his pipe into a metal ashtray and packed another pipe
load. "So did you ever tell her about your being in the Company?"

"No. She wasn't at all like Mom. She couldn't, wouldn't have
been able to keep her mouth shut … about anything. I couldn't
trust her."

"When you went out on assignment and you had to make up
something, she didn't trust you… probably thought you were
cheating on her."

"You got that right!"

I thought I'd watch a little TV, before I went home, when my cell
phone went off. It was the hospital. A nurse told me, hesitatingly,
that my dad had expired a few minutes ago.

The following morning, I called John Nelson, "This is Robert
Lombardi, I changed my mind about selling the house. I've decided
to move in, myself."

"Wha, wha, what about your job in La Crosse?"

"Screw La Crosse! I quit!" I waited for him to process my
statement before he hung up.

reathlessly, the Prime Minister scuttles down a long, wide hallway and reaches the King's chambers. "Your Majesty," he says, softly, "you must wake up. We have an emergency at hand."

"Well, what is it that you wake me during a most pleasant sleep?" the King asks.

"I beg your pardon, but there is, what appears to be an invasion force approaching our home. It is known, via our sensors, that they are of an unknown design, of unknown origin, not an expeditionary force and are heavily armed with sophisticated offensive weapons."

"Help me out of bed. Here hold onto one of my tentacles. How many of them are there?"

"Eight by my count, your Excellency."

"Not my tentacles you fool! I meant how many invaders?"

"Approximately fifty black vessels traveling at a high rate of speed, Sire."

"How close are they now?"

"They are close, my Liege, less than two thousand sphincters."

"Why did you wait to tell me this? Never mind. I will have to make an announcement to my subjects. Open all communication channels and standby."

"It is done, your Majesty. You may make the announcement," the Prime Minister bows as he informs the King.

The King begins the announcement: "My dear people, do not be alarmed, but we are about to experience another invasion attempt. Where are they from? And what do they want? You may be asking. As you remember, we successfully repelled the Fallopian invaders with our advanced weapons systems. We dispatched the Scrotums, as well because of their inferior weapons. These aggressive, primitive races do not have a chance against us."

"We have our Defensive Shield which the Prime Minister will activate in a few minutes and their entire armada will be engulfed in a horrific ball of fire; their own weapons turned against them. I regret taking this measure, but the only way to confront an overt act of aggression is with a pre-emptive strike."

The King turns to the Prime Minister and says, "Open a short-range channel with the armada, in all known languages and mathematical equations."

"Yes, Sire," the Prime Minister replies.

The King speaks to the invasion force: "Attention invaders. You have entered the sovereignty of our peaceful home. You will be annihilated if you do not return to your own planet."

"Your Majesty," The Prime Minister interrupts, "they are not turning away and are now within a thousand sphincters of our atmosphere."

Angered, the King replies, "Activate the Defensive Shield!"

"Sire, please forgive me, but you may have forgotten that the Defensive Shield was mentioned a long time ago as a way to prevent our people from panicking."

"Panicking from what?"

"Against the overwhelming odds that our home will be utterly destroyed."

"Do you mean to tell me that the Defensive Shield is only a sham?"

"No, not entirely, your Highness. It's a destructive device that when triggered, our home will explode leaving nothing for the invaders."

"Yes, I suppose it is better to kill ourselves than to be enslaved, of which we would certainly be. Do you concur, Prime Minister?"

"I do, my gracious King. According to the law, we are required to obtain permission from your mother, the Queen."

"Well then, go get her permission and hurry!"

"I am afraid that the Queen, is busy laying eggs for her new brood."

"The Chancellor is next in line. Get his permission."

"I am sorry to inform you that he is also busy fertilizing the eggs before the shells harden."

"The old Chancellor, or the new one?"

"The old one, Sire."

"The old one? I thought he was dead."

"No, he is not, but he did suffer some serious injuries the last time he fertilized. The room was dark and the Queen, instead of biting his head off, instead took a chunk out of his ass."

"Fine. Then run and get his permission."

The Prime Minister returns moments later and says, "The Chancellor is dead, but the Queen who is very angry at the interruption, gave her permission."

"All right, initiate the ... what do I name this, Prime Minister?"

"Oh, my kindly King, you may still call it the Defensive Shield. I will begin the countdown now. It will be over in less than ..."

he visitors

n eighteen-wheeler jackknifed, bounded over the highway median and crushed the driver's side of his wife's small car which had been traveling in the opposite direction.

The Reverend David Thompson understood the precision of God's handiwork, that is, if God had anything to do with it at all. He had reason to doubt it when the police told him of the truck driver's high BAC. For every paranormal event, David thought, there always seems to be something normal behind it; some reasonable explanation. It didn't allay the fact, however that his wife was dead.

Some members of his congregation, perhaps only a handful, expected him to deliver his own wife's eulogy, but he had hired his old friend, a Baptist minister from across town to officiate.

Pastor Thompson, still strikingly handsome at fifty-two, was the subject of his female congregants' attraction. Both young and old were cloyingly attentive. Things worsened after his wife was killed and they soon were bringing food like hot dishes, lasagna and spaghetti to his home and telling him how thin he was getting. They wanted to share his loss with him and he wanted to grieve alone.

So, after five years in the affluent community of West Des Moines, David decided to check the monthly bulletin for vacancies in other ELCA churches. He found one in Dubuque and phoned. They said they were interested, but he first had to gain permission and wait for it from the ELCA powers.

Selling his house and giving its furnishings to the Salvation Army, he drove east.

Reverend Thompson was hired almost immediately at Calvary Lutheran Church. Because it was a poorer parish than his former one, he was offered a parsonage, which was a sparsely furnished, two-bedroom bungalow; this, in lieu of a higher salary. He'd be responsible for paying his own utility bills.

Thompson was told, by the church secretary, that four families of inherited wealth controlled the finances and therefore were mainly responsible for paying his salary. Several, had placed themselves in positions of power within the church and served on key committees. In the back of his mind, he had the feeling, that with a wave of a hand from these apparently tight-fisted people, he could be dismissed as quickly as he was hired.

He began his duties routinely officiating at weddings, which were few, and funerals, which were many, because it had older membership. And, of course, visits to nursing homes.

David had met and married his wife, Carol, twenty years before, while he was still in the seminary. He was a heavy drinker, but promised his wife that he'd quit before he was ordained.

Hungover from the night before, he took his vows and was ordained. Now, with his wife gone, he took up the bottle again. A liter and a half of Windsor would last for four days.

Flat screen TV or a good book, his easy chair, feet up on the ottoman, three fingers of hooch and he was content.

One summer night, while watching TV, during an intense lightning storm, David thought he saw something shimmering, some shape illuminated against the wall. Was it a flash of lightning? Of course it was. But, there it was again and yet, again. He could discern, though blurred, two backlit, ethereal shapes; one large and one smaller. He blinked hard, but the shapes were still there. Draining his glass, snapping off the TV, he hurried to bed.

The following day, he was on his way to his church office, deep in thought about the event of the night before and attributed it to a Windsor hallucination.

"Pastor," an elderly woman, the permanent receptionist called, as he walked past. "Pastor, don't forget about the wedding this Saturday."

Jolted back to reality, "What wedding?"

"The Krauthammer-Anderson wedding. Second for each. Eleven o'clock."

"Oh yeah, the mixed marriage."

"What?"

"Never mind. Any calls for me?"

"No."

"I'll be in my office working on Sunday's sermon."

The day went as quickly as the torn, cotton clouds fled to the east. There wouldn't be any lightning storms that night.

TV and a couple or three glasses of the world's best anesthetic, was on David's evening agenda. After the news, he settled in earnest to watch an old movie. Then it happened.

A form, more defined than the previous night, though still slightly diaphanous, came toward him. It appeared to be a young girl, twelve maybe. The image wavered, but he could make out what she was wearing; a light blue, high-necked dress, nearly touching the floor and a large red bow holding a ponytail of blond hair. He catapulted to his feet.

"Mama, Mama! Oh God, Mama!"

The girl's mother turned from the pies she was baking, "What's the matter? Oh, you're as white as a ghost! What happened?"

"I'm so dizzy, Mama."

Her mother steadied her with hands on the girl's shoulders.

"Is it your time, Christina?"

"No, it's not that. In the dining room ..."

"What about the dining room?"

"There was a man! I could see him! Not clearly, but I could see him! He was tall and dressed strangely! Tan trousers and dark shirt!"

"Take another look, child. There's nothing there except chairs and a table. I'll give you a cold cloth to put on your forehead. You can lie down in your room 'til your father comes home. Meanwhile, I'll set the table for the guests we're having tonight."

David lurched across the deep pile carpeting, toward the wall, narrowly avoiding the ottoman and, with his hands felt the solidity of the wall. Was this the same girl, or whatever it was, that he saw last night? Did he really see anything? He returned to his chair, had another drink and recalled that she was wearing what appeared to be clothing from the early part of the last century, much like the family photographs he'd seen of ancient relatives. And when she put her hands to her mouth, was she stifling a scream?

Was she a … a ghost? No, no! His religious beliefs vigorously denied the idea. Furthermore, he would not, could not share this experience with anyone else.

Wait a minute, didn't Einstein, or some other physicist say that time is fluid? That the past exists simultaneously with the present? No, there is no present since time is moving forward and never stands still. This line of reasoning was giving David a headache, but he pushed on until he could reach a logical conclusion. He poured himself another drink. Ten minutes later, he passed out in the chair.

When he woke, it was morning. David no longer had the church ladies bringing him breakfast, so he had to make something himself. Then he would return to his time-space theories. Did the past overlap, somehow, with his time? Was it a tear in time itself which opened a sort of portal? Was he obsessing about some vision he saw while in a drunken delirium? The possibility presented itself to David. But it was so real! He asked God about it, but God remained mute.

Several weeks passed and no apparitions. The obsession stayed with him … to a lesser degree.

With church business concluded for the day, David drove to a neighboring town to buy a bottle of Windsor and planned to settle into his chair with a novel he'd begun to read. Suddenly a doorway opened in the wall and the girl appeared. Behind her, he could see a kitchen. It occurred to him that it was a portal; a doorway between her kitchen and his living room. She walked toward him and smiled faintly. Unthreatened, he smiled back. Her mouth moved, as if speaking, but he couldn't hear anything. Then she turned, still looking at David and reached for, what looked like someone else standing in the kitchen. A taller, mature woman was taken by the hand of the girl and apprehensively stepped forward. The girl's mouth was moving again and again, nothing audible. The woman was dressed similarly to the girl. David thought they could be Mother and Daughter. The woman also had blond hair, a little darker than her daughter's and had her hair done-up in a pompadour and she was very attractive. He moved toward them, they moved back and disappeared.

This was a more pleasant experience, David thought. They were making what could be called, progress and it called for a drink.

"Is this what the two of you do while I'm working all day? Seeing ghosts?"

"There's only one, Papa and he usually sits in the dining room."

"There's nobody in there! Anna, are you putting her up to this?"

"No, Joe, I've seen him too."

"Well then, you're both crazy! Now, I don't want to hear any more talk about this. Do you understand?"

"Yes, Papa."

"Yes, Joe."

The next morning, David phoned the church office and the secretary picked up. "Mrs. Wilson? I'm not coming in today. I've got some things to do around the house."

"Okay, Pastor."

Hearing that Mrs. Wilson, a true church lady, knew everything there was to know regarding the history of the church, he wondered if she knew anything about the parsonage and if there ever existed an older house on the same property.

"Yes and yes," she answered. "The house you're living in now, was built by a member of our church in the 1960's for a woman the man was engaged to, but when she broke off the engagement, she was Catholic, you know, and he didn't want to turn so, he gave the house to the church."

"Yes, but what about the older house?"

"Their name was Ackerson. Now, I don't usually like to spread gossip, but something, folks say, terrible really horrible happened in that house."

"What do you mean, horrible?"

"Hold on, I've got another call."

"Wait ... Mrs. Wilson!"

She put David on hold for only three minutes, but it seemed like thirty.

"Yes, Pastor Thompson. What was I talking about?"

"The old house."

"Not much more to tell except something really bad happened there. It was demolished right away. You might want to check it out at the library, or the Hall of Records at the courthouse. Is there anything else I can help you with?"

"No, I think that covers it. Thank you. I was just curious."

A couple of nights and a couple of Windsor's later, the doorway opened in the wall again and this time, a fat and balding man appeared, wearing a celluloid collar with a string tie, celluloid shirt cuffs with sleeve garters, his face crimson with rage, headed toward David, with clenched fists, mouth opening and closing rapidly. David thought he was so comical, he began to laugh.

"You must be Mr. Ackerson," David said.

The man stopped abruptly, threw his hands up and withdrew into his kitchen.

"Anna, are you, or are you not having an affair with that man?"

"Joe, I ... "

"Papa, she can't do anything with a ghost."

"Shut up. I'll deal with you later."

"Well, Anna?"

Two days followed. While David was fixing breakfast, the wall began glowing and the doorway opened. The girl and her mother stood in the doorway with looks of terror on their faces, their arms outstretched. This time he went to them and neither shrank back. He touched the mother's hand. It was surprisingly real and ... warm. He could even hear them talking! They pleaded for his help as they tried to pull him into their kitchen, which now had an eerie, orange glow reflecting on the walls.

"You've got to help us! He's a madman! Help us get out of here, please!"

They pulled harder, but David resisted. He jerked away, started stumbling on the thick carpet and fell. He started crawling on his hands and knees. They grabbed his legs and ankles and pulled him back across to the doorway.

When Pastor David Thompson neither showed up at church, nor did he call, Mrs. Wilson called the police and asked them to check on her pastor.

"Has he done anything like this before, Mrs. Wilson? Maybe he went out shopping or something."

"He would've called me! Please go over there."

"We'll send someone."

Two beefy officers answered the call. They knocked. No response.

"Put your shoulder to it," one of them said.

"It's unlocked, you moron! Hmm, maybe he stepped out."

"Well, he's not here."

"Obviously. Check the bedroom."

"His bed's not made."

"Whaja expect, he lives alone. Doesn't hafta impress anybody."

"Hey, look at this carpet. It looks like something heavy was dragged across it, right up to the wall and look at the carpet ... scorched on the edge, at the wall."

"Aw c'mon. What're you buckin' for? Detective? It's just another missing person report."

Had Reverend David Thompson gone to the Hall of Records, he could've discovered what had happened to the old house and what was so horrible about it. He would've reviewed the newspaper coverage, on microfiche, for that February of 1911.

Joe Ackerson's haberdashery business hadn't been doing well, due to a competitor's lower prices and he was growing more despondent by the day. The house had burned to the ground. Dubuque's all-volunteer fire department couldn't save it.

Joe Ackerson's body, untouched by the fire, was found in the cellar. He had set the house on fire then, hanged himself. Anna Ackerson and her daughter, Christina, had burned to death and were found in the kitchen. There was another body; an unidentified man lying next to them.

about the author

J. P. Johnson is a semi-retired real estate agent and is now living a work-optional lifestyle in Minneapolis, Minnesota, with his wife, Marylee and daughter, Erin. He is a long-time member of the Minneapolis Writers' Workshop.

Lost Lake Folk Art

SHIPWRECKT BOOKS PUBLISHING COMPANY

Minnesota